IN YOUR SHOES

ALSO BY DONNA GEPHART

Lily and Dunkin

As if Being 12 ¾ Isn't Bad Enough,
My Mother Is Running for President!

How to Survive Middle School

Olivia Bean, Trivia Queen

Death by Toilet Paper

Donna Gephart

IN YOUR SHOES

Delacorte Press

Text copyright © 2018 by Donna Gephart
Jacket art copyright © 2018 by Chris Silas Neal

All rights reserved. Published in the United States by Delacorte Press, an imprint of Random House Children's Books, a division of Penguin Random House LLC, New York.

Delacorte Press is a registered trademark and the colophon is a trademark of Penguin Random House LLC.

Visit us on the Web! rhcbooks.com

Educators and librarians, for a variety of teaching tools, visit us at RHTeachersLibrarians.com

Library of Congress Cataloging-in-Publication Data is available upon request.
ISBN 978-1-5247-1373-7 (hc) — ISBN 978-1-5247-1375-1 (ebook)

The text of this book is set in 13-point Apollo.
Interior design by Trish Parcell

Printed in the United States of America
10 9 8 7 6 5 4 3 2 1
First Edition

Dedicated to Dan—
From our first date, you really bowled me over, babe.
I'm sorry about "accidentally" throwing out
your old bowling shoes.

Life on earth is such a good story
you cannot afford to miss the beginning. . . .
                                        –Lynn Margulis

Some stories start with "Once upon a time . . ."

Some start with a dramatic moment, like the appearance of a meteor hurtling toward Earth.

Stories can be plenty dramatic without a meteor. As I'm sure you know, while we're living our ordinary lives in ordinary places, Earth is spinning 1,000 miles per hour on its axis. That seems pretty dramatic to me.

While Earth spins and orbits the sun, this particular story starts in one of those ordinary places—Buckington, Pennsylvania.

At the start of this story, there's a nervous boy who braves freezing temperatures to get to his favorite place in the universe.

And there's a grieving girl who wakes in a new bedroom somewhere she hadn't meant to be.

There's also a nosy, noisy narrator—Me!—intruding now and again to direct your attention to things that matter deeply.

So this story absolutely does not begin with "Once upon a time . . ." or with a meteor hurtling toward Earth.

It starts (and ends) with a bowling shoe.

As these things sometimes do.

FRAME 1	FRAME 2	FRAME 3	FRAME 4	FRAME 5
FRAME 1	FRAME 2	FRAME 3	FRAME 4	FRAME 5
FRAME 1	FRAME 2	FRAME 3	FRAME 4	FRAME 5
FRAME 1	FRAME 2	FRAME 3	FRAME 4	FRAME 5
FRAME 1	FRAME 2	FRAME 3	FRAME 4	FRAME 5
FRAME 1	FRAME 2	FRAME 3	FRAME 4	FRAME 5
FRAME 1	FRAME 2	FRAME 3	FRAME 4	FRAME 5
FRAME 1	FRAME 2	FRAME 3	FRAME 4	FRAME 5

FRAME ONE

If the Shoe Fits, Throw It

Miles

Miles Spagoski jogged the four blocks to his family's bowling center, shivering and imagining ways he might die—a frozen tree limb could crack off and land on his head, a distracted driver fiddling with a car's heating controls could swerve onto the sidewalk and plow him flat, or, if he was outside long enough, plain old hypothermia could be the end of his short, sad story.

But the moment Miles entered Buckington Bowl, his worries melted away like snowflakes on a warm palm. Miles relaxed, as much as someone like him could relax, onto a stool behind the front counter and kicked off his worn sneakers.

He loved his family's bowling center first thing in

the morning, before his dad put the oldies rock station on to play through the crackly speaker system, before pins crashed on lanes 1 through 48, before video games near the snack counter beeped and blinked and beckoned. Before—

"Hey, Spagoski!" Randall Fleming yelled through the thick glass doors, startling Miles. Backpack slung over one shoulder, face pressed against the glass where the painted words read "No gum allowed in this building," Randall made smudges with his mouth and pounded the door with a gloved fist. "Open up. My snot's freezing."

Miles unlocked the automatic doors for his best friend to slip through. He'd tried to make Randall call him by his first name, but there were *five* other Mileses in their grade, so Randall insisted on "Spagoski" for specificity. He was stubborn like that.

"Why didn't you open up sooner?" Randall blinked, blinked, blinked. "My eyeballs were turning into ice cubes out there."

"It's not *that* cold." Miles reached behind the counter and grabbed Windex and a rag. "Why'd you have to slobber all over the door? You know I have to clean that."

Randall shrugged. Miles went outside in his socks to quickly wipe the smudges off the glass, then darted back in, shivering again. "It's fr-fr-freezing! Feels like the temperature dropped twenty degrees since I got here."

"Told you," Randall said, stamping his brand-new sneakers, even though there wasn't any snow on the ground. "They should cancel school today and give us one more day of winter vacation."

Miles imagined spending the whole day bowling. He'd take his first break at lunch when his dad started grilling in the bowling center's kitchen. And when Miles's arm got sore from rolling so many strikes, he'd hang out with the regulars, like Stick, who'd teach him the finer points of playing pool so Miles could hustle kids at the pool table as well as on the lanes, and Tyler, the mechanic, who would take him back behind the lanes and let him help fix things when they broke down, which was often. It would be a perfect day. "They should cancel school for the rest of winter," Miles said. "We could bowl like eight games a day every day. Imagine how high our averages would get."

"They should cancel that dumb school dance." Randall kicked at nothing. "Did you see the way Marcus Lopez asked Lacey Smith to the dance before break? That idiot hid a dozen roses in her locker and then had Mr. Cedeno ask her for him over the morning announcements."

1

"Yeah, that was crazy," Miles said. "What if she said no?"

"Right. But of course she said yes. Way to raise the bar for the rest of us, Marcus."

Both boys laughed, but Miles wasn't laughing on the inside. He knew the dumb dance was another thing he'd worry about. Would he find someone to ask? How would he ask her in a big way without embarrassing himself? Would she say yes? He didn't have the popularity power of Marcus Lopez. And he didn't even like dancing. You could get bumped into, stepped on, rejected, made fun of. Too much unpredictability. Miles liked bowling, where things made sense. You rolled a heavy ball down a wooden lane in an attempt to knock over ten pins. Simple. Fun. Predictable. Nothing terrible ever happened in bowling. Even the dreaded gutter ball wasn't the end of the world. There was always the next roll or the next game. Always a chance for a do-over.

If only life were more like bowling.

Miles ducked behind the counter, put the Windex away, and switched on lane 48. He handed Randall a pair of size 11 bowling shoes, marveling at how much bigger Randall's feet were than his own. Miles grabbed the handle of his black wheeled bowling bag. "You're lucky you can ask Tate," Miles said. "I can't think of one girl at Buckington Middle who'd want to go with me."

8

"Aw. Come on." Randall flung his arm around Miles's shoulders and squeezed. "There's got to be one girl who's desperate enough to go with you, Spagoski. You know, someone with really bad vision who wouldn't realize how ugly you are."

Miles wriggled out of Randall's grip. He decided to think about bowling, not girls, not the dumb dance and definitely not Randall's unfunny comment. He thought if he did everything right this morning, maybe he'd bowl his first perfect game.

Three hundred beautiful points. Twelve gorgeous strikes in a row.

His older sister, Mercedes, once told him some nine-year-old girl in Florida bowled a perfect game in league play. Miles figured if a nine-year-old could do it, he should be able to do it, too. He was three years older than that girl and probably had a lot more bowling experience, since his grandfather owned Buckington Bowl and his parents worked there.

But in all his years of playing, Miles had never bowled a perfect game.

If you believe in yourself and work hard enough, you can do anything, Miles's grandmother, Bubbie Louise, used to say. *Except bowl a 301. Even Superman can't do that, bubeleh . . . and he's got those cute tights and all.*

Miles still missed Bubbie Louise, even though she died a year ago, shortly after his eleventh birthday.

Miles knew he should be done missing her by now, but he couldn't help how he felt.

"I'm going to kick your bowling butt, Spagoski," Randall said as they walked toward lane 48.

Miles shook his head. "Yeah, well, Grandpop Billy gave me a new bowling ball for Chanukah, so I'm going to kick *your* butt today, Rand." Miles stretched his leg behind Randall to literally kick him in the butt, but since Randall was so much taller, Miles managed only a weak tap on the back of Randall's left thigh.

Miles made a mental note to himself: *Grow.*

"What's that pitiful move? This is a proper kick to the butt." And Randall kicked Miles's rear end so hard that Miles lurched forward, windmilling his arms to keep from face-planting onto the worn purple carpet—the one with images of bowling pins and colorful squares, triangles and circles. It was the same carpet Miles had learned his shapes and colors on when he was little.

Miles balanced himself, muttering, "Yeah, remind me why we're friends?"

Randall couldn't answer. He was laughing so hard he doubled over and started wheezing. Sometimes laughing too hard triggered coughing and wheezing for Randall. Other times, cold weather did it. Even a whiff of someone's perfume or stinky deodorant could make Randall's airways clog with mucus and set him wheezing for hours. The worst, though, was being around cats and dogs. They always triggered a full-blown wheeze-o-rama.

Randall took two quick puffs of medicine from his orange inhaler, and after a few breaths his airways relaxed and the raspy wheezes subsided.

"Who's makin' all that racket?" called a figure hunched over on a stool at the snack counter, his wheelchair behind him.

Both boys looked up, startled.

Miles's grandfather, Billy Spagoski, sat with a mug of steaming coffee in his chapped red hands. He was wearing his "Shut Up and Bowl" embroidered T-shirt. "You boys are having way too much fun for a Tuesday morning. Aren't you supposed to be in school?"

Don't remind us, Pop, Miles thought, remembering all the hours he'd be wasting at school when he could be on the lanes practicing.

"Hey there, Mr. Spagoski." Randall waved. "I'm about to kick your grandson's butt again."

Miles covered his backside with his hand in case Randall was being literal.

"Yeah, I'll bet you are," Grandpop Billy answered. "Just don't let him hustle you too badly, Randall."

Randall put a hand to his perfectly pressed button-down dress shirt, over his heart. "Miles? Hustle me? That boy couldn't swindle me in bowling if I had both hands tied behind my back. Hustle *me*? Miles? Ha!"

"Yeah, that's what I said," Billy called. "Miles. Hustle *you*! Got icicles stuck in your ears?"

Miles grabbed his friend's backpack strap and pulled. "Come on. We've got to hurry if we want to get in a game before school. I'm going to bowl a three hundred today. I feel it." Then he called, "I'm totally going to hustle him, Pop."

Grandpop Billy laughed and then muttered into his steaming coffee, "I swear, that boy is just like me."

At lane 48, Miles pulled his nearly new Blue Thunder Storm Crux ball from his bowling bag and thought about kissing it for luck but simply hoisted it onto the ball return. He didn't need luck. Miles had skill. The kind of skill that came from having practiced nearly every day since you were three and a half and you rolled your bowling ball down a purple plastic dinosaur-shaped ramp onto a lane flanked by bumpers.

Randall picked out a black, twelve-pound house ball and hurried to lane 48 to put on his bowling shoes, after carefully placing his new sneakers on a nearby chair.

"You got five bucks to bet on this one?" Miles asked.

"I've got ten." Randall tipped his chin up. "Sold an expensive pair of kicks to some dude in North Dakota yesterday. Cha-ching!"

"Awesome." Miles figured Randall spent most of the money he made selling sneakers online buying nice clothes and new sneakers for himself, but Miles managed to win some of that cha-ching on the lanes.

Both boys put their ten-dollar bills on the table.

When Miles tugged on the thick laces of his bowling shoes, he felt an unusual tingle radiate up his legs and through his body, like something magical was about to happen. "You're not ready for me today, Randall." Miles wiggled his toes inside his lucky bowling shoes. The shoes felt . . . perfect.

Randall walked toward the foul line, pulled his right arm back and swung the ball forward, ending with his signature single hop. When all ten pins fell, Randall leapt. "Told you! I'm gonna whomp your butt today, Spagoski! Boo-yah!"

Miles bowled a strike, too, but was quieter about it.

Randall, on his next turn, downed only three pins, then five, to lose the spare. Randall's following turn netted him seven pins and then only one more—another botched spare. "You guys need to oil these lanes better, or something."

Miles ignored Randall's remark and followed his first strike with two more.

"A turkey for a turkey!" Randall shouted.

Miles didn't respond to the insult because he knew Randall was trying to distract him from his strike streak. He decided to flip the distraction strategy back on his friend. When it was Randall's turn to bowl, Miles asked, "Did you hear about the guy who died from getting hit in his junk?"

Randall looked over his shoulder at Miles. "Is that a joke?"

"Nope. No joke."

"Good, 'cause that stuff ain't funny. Anyway, a guy can't die from that." Randall looked at Miles again. "But if it hurts bad enough, he might wish he could." Randall laughed, but it turned into a cough.

"It's true," Miles said. "I read about it last night. Dick Wertheim was hit—"

"Wait up." Randall, still cradling his bowling ball, pivoted. "What was this dude's first name?"

"Don't be dumb. It's short for Richard."

"Oh, yeah, I knew that." Randall finally took his turn. Signature hop. Five pins clattered down in the quiet of the bowling center. "You distracted me on purpose, Spagoski!"

"Did not," Miles said, even though he had. "You're just a lousy bowler, Rand. So anyway, this guy was hit by a tennis ball right in his, well, you know. Then he collapsed, hit his head on the ground and died. Died! It's like you could die from anything at any time. We could die right now." Miles felt that familiar racing heartbeat.

He forced himself to get up and take his turn anyway.

"We're not going to die right now. And that guy definitely didn't die from getting hit in the junk."

"Indirectly he did."

"No. He died from hitting his head on the ground."

Miles thought Randall would make an excellent lawyer someday. He was good at arguing. Or maybe he'd be an international business mogul. Randall made big bank buying and selling sneakers online.

"Why do you keep talking about such weird things all the time?" Randall asked, approaching the lane for his turn. "I don't think it's good for you."

Miles shrugged. "Thought it was interesting. That's all." But the truth was, Miles wondered the same thing: Why did he think weird ways people died was fascinating?

"You see that?" Randall screamed.

Miles hadn't seen.

"Aw, man, you weren't even looking. Why aren't you ever looking when I bowl a strike?"

"Sorry." Miles didn't tell his friend he was too busy thinking about death again to focus on his strike. Sometimes Miles wondered if maybe his obsession was keeping him from bowling a perfect game.

Seriously, Miles thought. *What is wrong with me?*

Amy

*W*hat is wrong with me? Amy Silverman wondered.

Sitting on the edge of the bed, wearing her first-day-at-a-new-school outfit of a blue-and-white-striped sweater, jeans and her black-and-lime-green sneakers, one of which had a heel lift, Amy checked her phone for the millionth time. She hoped for another text from her dad. He'd already wished her luck the night before, but it wasn't enough for Amy. She wanted him to be there with her.

Even her best friend, Kat, hadn't texted her yet this morning.

How was Amy supposed to face this day all by herself? She didn't even have her dog, Ernest, to keep her company and help her feel less nervous.

Amy allowed herself to fall back onto the bed. But the quilt smelled moldy, like it had been sitting at the back of an old closet for a hundred dusty years, so Amy sat up again. Just then, her phone vibrated in her hand.

Her heart thumped as she checked the new message.

It was a photo of Ernest with their former neighbor, Pam. Ernest and Pam were wearing matching sunglasses. Pam was grinning. Ernest looked annoyed.

The photo made Amy's stomach clench. It wasn't fair that Ernest was with Pam in Chicago while Amy was stuck in Borington—er, Buckington, Pennsylvania, without her dad. This wasn't how the story of her life was supposed to unfold. In one chapter, she was happy with her family in their Chicago apartment, and in the next—everything fell apart.

Every. Single. Thing.

How would Amy ever get her old life back?

She replied to Pam's message with a smiley face emoji wearing sunglasses because it was the perfect response. But Amy wasn't feeling smiley or cool like that emoji. She was angry and lonely and, if she was being completely honest, scared. What she really wanted to reply with was the poop emoji, because that's exactly how her life felt right now. Like one big poop emoji.

Amy fell backward onto the smelly bed again. She

wondered what would happen if she stayed there and skipped her first day at the new school. Would anyone notice?

"Breakfast!" Uncle Matt knocked on the bedroom door. "I made waffles today, Ames. Big first day at school and all."

Amy bolted up. She wasn't getting out of this.

"*Blueberry* waffles!" Uncle Matt yelled from the other side of the door, as though they were the most exciting thing since modern embalming techniques were invented.

Amy's dad had always made waffles for breakfast on big days, like the first day of summer vacation or when her mom got the job with the post office several years ago. Waffles were *his* specialty, especially blueberry ones.

Everything felt wrong today.

"Ames?"

"Be there in a minute," she managed to say.

"Huh?" Uncle Matt knocked on the door again. "Can't hear you, Ames."

Amy took a sharp breath. "Be right there!" Then she let all the air leak out of her, felt a hot tear snake down her right cheek and smooshed a thin, gray-covered pillow over her face.

The pillow smelled like mold, too.

A Good Mistake

As Miles and Randall walked toward the front counter, Grandpop Billy called, "How much did he hustle you for, kid?"

Randall inhaled deeply, a soft wheeze rattling. "Ten bucks."

"Warned ya."

"You did," Randall called. "See you later, Mr. Spagoski."

"Have a good day, Pop!" Miles called. "Hey, you need anything before we go?" Before he left the bowling center, Miles always made sure his grandfather had everything he needed. It wasn't so easy for his grandpop to get around with the terrible thing that happened to his legs from the accident all those years ago.

"Nah, I'm fine. Get to school, you hoodlums."

"Will do, Pop. See you later."

Miles placed his bowling bag behind the counter and squirted some disinfectant spray in Randall's bowling shoes. He'd once read there are 250,000 sweat glands in a pair of feet, which is gross. Plus, his mom told him he had to spray every pair of shoes before they went back on the shelves, even his friends' shoes. Especially friends' shoes! Miles placed the giant pair of shoes on the shelf and grabbed his winter jacket and backpack.

Then he looked at Grandpop Billy, bent over at his spot at the snack counter. Miles's heart gave a tug. He touched the ten-dollar bills in his pocket and nodded. Miles had almost enough money for the big gift for his grandfather's seventy-fifth birthday. It was going to be the trip of a lifetime for a guy who owns a bowling center—an all-expenses-paid vacation to the International Bowling Museum and Hall of Fame in Arlington, Texas.

"Let's go," Randall said, walking backward toward the doors.

The boys walked out into the blustery parking lot.

"Hey, guys!" Miles's dad, George Spagoski, called from the bright-orange Buckington Bowl van. The one with the giant fake bowling ball and pins on the roof.

The one that looked like a fat pumpkin on wheels. Mr. Spagoski hopped out of the driver's seat and turned his collar up to cover the back of his neck. His thick, chapped fingers were wrapped around a paper cup of coffee from Wawa.

"Dad." Miles nodded.

"Mr. S," Randall said, wiping his nose.

"You guys heading to—?" Mr. Spagoski looked down and his shoulders sagged. "Miles, you forgot to change out of your bowling shoes."

Surprised, Miles looked at his feet. "Oh, man!" His sneakers were in his bowling bag, behind the counter. He'd never forgotten to change out of his shoes before. What had happened today? Was his mind too cluttered with worries?

"You can't wear those shoes back on the lanes," Miles's dad said. "The grit and dirt from the ground will scratch the wood."

"I know. I know." Miles shifted his backpack onto his other shoulder. "I have another pair at home I can wear on the lanes. But these are my lucky shoes. I get better scores when I wear these." Miles got a pang of sadness that he wouldn't be able to wear his favorite bowling shoes again on the lanes, but then he remembered his score and that he won ten bucks from Randall. "Hey, Dad, I just bowled a one-eighty."

Miles's dad gave him a fist bump. "That's terrific." He took a noisy slurp of coffee. "Inching closer to that perfect game."

"You know it," Miles said. He looked down at his bowling shoes and felt that strange tingling sensation again.

Randall nudged Miles with his shoulder. "Come on. We gotta go."

"Yeah. Later, Dad."

"Aren't you going to change into sneakers now?" his dad asked.

"Yeah," Randall said. "Aren't you?"

Something inside Miles's brain snapped like a rubber band. These were his lucky bowling shoes, but maybe they'd be lucky outside the lanes, too. It wasn't like he could wear them on the lanes again anyway. Maybe, like a powerful talisman, they'd keep something horrible from happening to him. Maybe they'd be a lucky charm to help him get a girl to go to the dumb dance with him. "Nope," Miles said. "I'm going to wear these today."

"To school?" his dad asked. Another noisy slurp of coffee. "You're going to wear bowling shoes to *school*?"

"I am." Miles imagined some girl finding him interesting because of the shoes, and he got a dreamy look in his eyes.

Randall looked horrified, or maybe his facial features had just frozen that way.

"Suit yourself," Miles's dad said. "Just don't wear 'em back on the lanes."

"I won't." Miles shifted his backpack again and shivered from the cold. "I don't want to scratch the lanes. I'm not an idiot."

"No, you're not." His dad walked toward the doors of the bowling center, holding his coffee out in front of him. "But you're weird. You know that. Right?"

"You look like a dork with those shoes," Randall said as they walked toward school. "More specifically, you're going to look like a dork near me, which will make me look like a dork by association."

"Dork by Association? Sounds like the name of a band." Miles reached up and hit Randall in the chest with the back of his gloved hand. "Believe me, you're tall, dork and *not* handsome without my help." Miles knew this wasn't true. Randall was the Sultan of Style and wouldn't be seen dead wearing bowling shoes outside of the lanes. "Besides," Miles said, "I'm thinking these shoes might be a way to get a date for the dance."

Randall slowed for a second and then glared at Miles. "Explain."

Miles's mouth wasn't working so well because of the below-freezing temperatures, but he managed to say, "Some guys get tattoos. R-r-r-right? Some dye their hair purple. You know, like it's their s-s-s-signature thing. It makes them quirky cool. My signature thing is going to be w-w-w-wearing bowling shoes. Perfect. Right? Why didn't I think of this before?"

"Because it's dorky, Miles." Randall wiped his nose with the back of his gloved hand. "Painfully, horribly, get-your-head-shoved-in-a-toilet dorky. *My* signature thing is wearing cool kicks, so I don't want you messing up my vibe. It's bad enough when you wear those ratty-looking, tired sneakers, but these shoes? Uh-uh. Don't you know anything about style, Spagoski?"

"You're just jealous." Miles's feet were freezing inside the bowling shoes, but he didn't mention it. "People will think I'm cooler than you for wearing something so different."

Randall turned and punched Miles in the shoulder.

"What?" Miles asked.

"You're an idiot. And I don't want people to see me with you if you're going to wear those stupid bowling shoes to school. They're fine on the lanes, but—"

"Bowling. Shoes. Are. NOT. Stupid. You are!" Miles thought about his grandfather, who, Miles imagined, wished he could don a pair of bowling shoes, but that was pretty hard to do when you didn't have the bottom parts of your legs. Miles's whole body filled with rage at the unfairness of life. He faced Randall, planted his feet and looked down at his multicolored shoes with the thick white laces. "Bowling shoes are awesome!" Miles may have spit on Randall a little when he yelled. Then, poking Randall in the chest with a gloved finger, Miles delivered his final shot: "Tate McAllister will probably think they're so hot she'll want to make out with me."

"*Excuse you?* What'd you say?"

"Thought you didn't want to be late for school?"

Randall shoved Miles hard with two flat palms against his chest.

Miles stumbled backward. He planted his bowling shoes again, steadied himself and blinked, shocked that his best friend would do that. Then Miles wielded his words like weapons: "I said she'll want to make—"

Randall didn't let Miles finish. He charged into him with all the force his skinny bag-o'-bones body could muster, searing anger sizzling through the frosty air between them.

F(l)ight

The two boys dropped like bowling pins at the masterful hand of the late bowling great Billy Hardwick.

"Get off!" Miles screamed. "The grass is fr-fr-freezing my butt."

"Apologize!"

"There's people, Rand. Get off me!"

"Apologize for what you said about . . . Tate."

"I didn't say anything. Just that she'll want to—"

"Aaaahhhhhhh!" Randall had swiveled and grabbed for Miles's feet. He pulled his own glove off with his teeth, then managed to untie and yank off Miles's right bowling shoe. All the while, Miles pounded gloved fists on Randall's back, screaming, "She'll want to make out with me! She'll want to make out with me! She'll love my bowling shoes!"

Randall rocketed up, holding Miles's bowling shoe high, like a trophy. "Is this it?" He was panting and wheezing. "This what she'll love so much?"

"Give it!" Miles yelled, and leapt for the shoe. His socked foot froze instantly.

Randall held the blue, red and vomit-beige* bowling shoe even higher, out of Miles's reach. "Say you're sorry."

A couple kids walked by, gawking at the odd duo.

Miles hopped on the foot that still had a bowling shoe on it. "You're a jerk!" he screamed once the kids had passed. "Give my shoe back before I—"

"Say it, Miles, and I'll give it back. Say it!"

Miles screamed toward the sky: "Bowling shoes will definitely make Tate McAllister want to make out with me!"

Snorting like a wild bull, Randall pulled his arm back and flung Miles's bowling shoe upward with what seemed like superhuman strength. Then he took a couple squirts from his inhaler.

The bowling shoe took flight as though it had wings. It made a poetic arc against the cloud-spattered sky.

---

* Vomit-beige should be a new crayon color. Could you please work on that, Crayola?

Bowling is all physics and energy distribution. It's
F = ma. So it is actually one of the most science-y
sports, because it literally is just a ball and a surface
and objects to knock down. —CHRIS HARDWICK

If you know anything about Isaac Newton's three laws of motion, and I'm sure you do, you realize one of two things happened next.

Thing 1: Gravity did what it does best and exerted its force on the bowling shoe and pulled it to Earth. *Thunk.*

No story.

Thing 2: Something got in the way of the trajectory of the bowling shoe at the tail end of its wild arc and stopped its forward momentum. *Blam! Thud.*

BIG story.

Thing 2, of course, is what happened.

Some*thing* didn't get in the way of Miles's red, blue and vomit-beige bowling shoe. Some*one* got in the way.

But it wasn't her fault.

(Even without getting all science-y, Isaac Newton could have figured that out.)

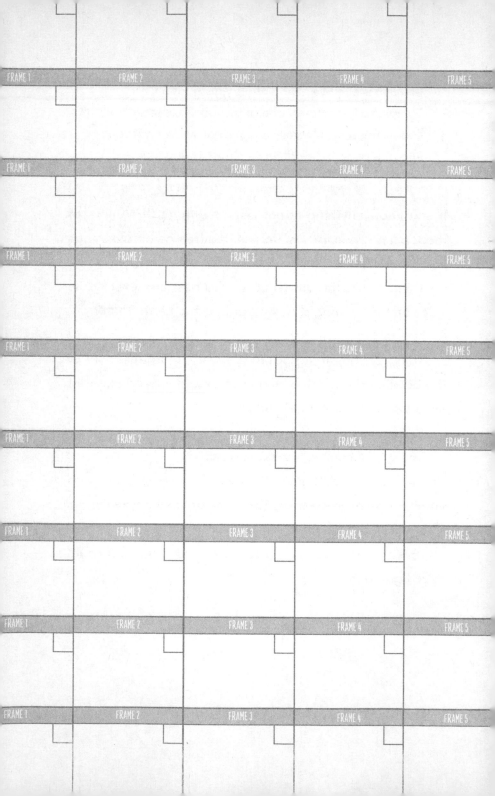

FRAME 1 FRAME 2 FRAME 3 FRAME 4 FRAME 5

FRAME 1 FRAME 2 FRAME 3 FRAME 4 FRAME 5

FRAME 1 FRAME 2 FRAME 3 FRAME 4 FRAME 5

FRAME 1 FRAME 2 FRAME 3 FRAME 4 FRAME 5

FRAME 1 FRAME 2 FRAME 3 FRAME 4 FRAME 5

FRAME 1 FRAME 2 FRAME 3 FRAME 4 FRAME 5

FRAME 1 FRAME 2 FRAME 3 FRAME 4 FRAME 5

FRAME 1 FRAME 2 FRAME 3 FRAME 4 FRAME 5

FRAME TWO

Footwear Meets Forehead

FRAME 6   FRAME 10

FRAME 6   FRAME 10

FRAME 6   FRAME 10

FRAME 6   FRAME 7   FRAME 8   FRAME 9   FRAME 10

FRAME 6   FRAME 7   FRAME 8   FRAME 9   FRAME 10

FRAME 6   FRAME 7   FRAME 8   FRAME 9   FRAME 10

Amy, the Hero of Her Own Story

*K*erchunk!

The heel of the shoe connected soundly with Amy Silverman's forehead.

Like universes colliding.

Like two unrelated stories connecting.

Like fate, forehead and flying footwear had come together in exactly the way they needed to.

But for the moment and without the gift of insight, foresight and second sight, Amy was simply and significantly shocked. Why would someone do this to her? Especially on her first day at a new school? Weren't things hard enough for her already?

From the force of impact, Amy was thrown backward onto her bottom, legs straight out in front of her, hot tears stinging her nearly frozen eyes.

There was a bowling shoe on the pavement near her. *A bowling shoe?*

Amy felt a sudden, fierce longing. Surprisingly, it wasn't for her mom, but for her dog Ernest, who surely would have protected her from the bizarre flying object. Ernest, who, Amy was positive, did not enjoy wearing silly sunglasses for stupid selfies. Ernest, who would leap into Amy's lap and lick her face no matter what had happened. Ernest, who was the kindest, most loyal corgi ever to walk the Earth on four fine, furry paws. Ernest, who was unceremoniously given to their neighbor Pam before Amy and her dad moved 765 miles from Chicago, Illinois, to Buckington, Pennsylvania. Because, for Pete's sake, you couldn't possibly have a dog when you lived in a—

"Hey!"

Two boys ran toward Amy. Well, the tall one ran, and the other one, arms flailing, limped/hopped.

Amy would notice that.

Ignoring the throbbing in her forehead, Amy quickly tucked her right foot underneath her, hiding her black-and-lime-green sneaker with the two-centimeter heel lift. The extra rubber at the bottom of her right sneaker made her look weird, she knew, but she also knew those sneakers had been a gift from her mom—an expensive gift. She instantly hated herself for doing that and stuck her leg out in front again. Her mom wouldn't have wanted her to hide that part of herself—her leg-length discrepancy, the reason she was slightly shorter on her right side.

Amy could have worn inserts inside her sneakers, where no one would see them, and she did that for a while. But after her mom died, Amy pulled the sneakers from the back of her closet. She decided to honor her mom and wear them proudly every day. Let people stare!

The tall boy skidded up first. "Oh my . . . Are you . . . ? I can't believe—"

"You're bleeding!" the other boy shrieked. "Your head, it's—it's—bleeding!"

"I'm really sorry," the tall one said. "It was—"

"All your fault!" the other boy yelled, shoving the tall one.

The tall one shoved him back.

Amy scooted away from the fray. A single drop of her blood plopped onto the sidewalk. It reminded Amy of Sleeping Beauty when she pricked her finger on the spindle. "Hey, do you guys have a tissue or something? Oh my gosh. I can't believe . . ." Nothing was working out like it was supposed to. Her first day at a new school was not supposed to go this way. When Amy imagined the story outline of this day, it did *not* involve a bowling shoe and these two charac-ters. *Truth really is stranger than fiction,* Amy thought.

The boy who'd been putting his bowling shoe back on fished awkwardly in his jacket pockets and handed over a small piece of paper. "It's all I have."

"Never mind," Amy said, shoving the piece of paper into her pocket. "I'm good." There was no way she was pressing that grimy piece of paper to her fore-head. "You can stop staring now," she said from her spot on the ground.

The whole thing made Amy feel like crying, but she'd promised herself she wouldn't cry again today. Of course, when she'd made that promise, she couldn't have anticipated being clonked in the forehead by a flying bowling shoe.

"Come on. She's good," the tall boy said. "Let's go. We're going to be late."

"But . . . ," the other boy said. "We can't leave her sitting there like that."

"Please," Amy said. "Leave me sitting here. Really. I want you to go."

So they went.

The tall boy ran toward school, his backpack bouncing against his spine.

The other boy ran after him. But he stopped and looked back at Amy, his eyes wide. Then he continued on. "Wait, Randall! I have to tell you something!"

"What?" the tall boy yelled.

"I'm sorry! I shouldn't have said that about . . ."

Amy wondered what Bowling Shoe Boy was sorry about and what he shouldn't have said. Her writer brain was always paying attention to details, like the moment the boy stopped and looked back at her. Amy figured he couldn't believe what a weirdo she was, sitting on the cold ground, bleeding and not getting up. He probably noticed the heel lift at the bottom of her right sneaker, too.

Oh, how Amy longed to rewrite this morning.

She wished she'd been allowed to stay home and spend the day in her room, writing. Not that she liked where she was living now, but she could have lost herself in creating a story. She would have been transported to a different world, maybe a castle from centuries ago, maybe a peasant's hut in a beautiful part of Ireland, maybe—

An icy wind sliced through Amy, making her shiver as though she weren't wearing a winter coat. Since she wasn't allowed to stay home and write, maybe she'd remain there on the ground and freeze to death, like the Little Match Girl from the fairy tale her mom used to read her.

Get up, sweets. You're not going to let a little thing like an airborne bowling shoe hold you back. Are you?

Amy shook her head in answer. She loved when her

37

mom's voice floated into her head. It seemed to come when she needed it most, and it made her feel less alone, more brave. Her mom's words reminded Amy that, every now and again, life had a way of kicking your legs out from underneath you, then daring you to stand back up.

Amy stood back up.

She brushed off the seat of her pants and let out a forceful, frosty breath. She was numb from the cold. Her forehead throbbed. Yet she was ready to face this day. She could do it, even with a fresh cut on her forehead. After all, Amy was the hero of her own story. Wasn't she?

And this unexpected incident? It was merely a plot twist—a surprising turn of events in her life story.

Plot twists could be fun.

But, really.

A flying bowling shoe?

Maybe it was more than a plot twist, Amy thought. *Maybe it was an inciting incident.* Her forehead tingled, and the tingle radiated through her whole body. She knew that an "inciting incident" meant the beginning of something new, something big, something that made the protagonist act whether they wanted to or not. An inciting incident meant things changed in some irrevocable way, and she couldn't go back to how things were before. Of course, Amy despised the last inciting incident in her life—the one that changed everything for the worse—but maybe this one would be positive. Perhaps this inciting incident was packed with promise and possibility.

Amy hurried to school, excited to see what lay ahead.

The Nice Nurse

In the quiet hallway of Buckington Middle School, a man who wore a name badge that read *Vice Principal Cedeno* said to Amy, "You're late for homeroom!" He squinted. "Hey, what happened to your head?"

Amy reached up and touched her forehead. Her fingers came away sticky wet. "I . . . I . . ." There was no way she could tell him a bowling shoe fell from the sky and hit her in the head. He wouldn't believe her. If it hadn't happened to Amy, she wouldn't believe it herself. "I ran into a door."

"Ouch." He pointed down the hall. "Go to the nurse's room and get the cut cleaned up, then get a late pass from the main office."

Amy went.

Inciting incident, Amy reminded herself as she walked down the hall toward the sign that read Nurse's Office. Her life story might be about to take a dramatic turn. At least she hoped it would.

The nurse's office was a bright, warm room that smelled like Amy's doctor's office back in Chicago—a faint odor of medicine, rubbing alcohol and hand sanitizer. Amy wondered who her new doctors would be here in Buckington and how they'd handle her leg-length discrepancy. Her old doctor wanted to wait until she was done growing to see if the bone in her right thigh corrected itself. Amy hoped it did, so she wouldn't need surgery and could stop wearing sneakers with a bulky heel lift. She just wanted to be like everyone else.

Oh, you'll never be like everyone else, sweets. And isn't that a wonder-filled thing?

Amy smiled at the sound of her mom's words in her mind. She hung on to them as if they were oxygen, not realizing how much she needed to hear them, not realizing how nervous she felt standing in the nurse's office in this new school with a pulsing, aching cut on her forehead.

"What do we have here?" the nurse asked, breaking the spell Amy was under from the soft sound of her mom's voice.

The nurse wore black slacks, black clogs with rainbow-striped socks, and a pink lab coat over a long-sleeved black top. Her hair was pulled back into a tight ponytail. She wore an ID tag on a lanyard around her neck. "Tell me what happened to your head."

"I . . . uh . . . walked into the edge of a door."

The nurse gently examined Amy's forehead. "Were you looking at your phone? Kids are always getting hurt doing that."

"No. Just clumsy, I guess." Amy decided her story sounded believable, even though it wasn't true. Amy wasn't clumsy. She was graceful despite her leg-length discrepancy. In fact, she loved to dance. It was the one thing besides writing that allowed her to transcend time and place. To her, dancing was another form of expression—and that expression was usually of pure happiness. It was no surprise that she hadn't danced—not once—since her mom died.

When her mom was well, Amy and she had danced together in their tiny kitchen while they cooked dinner. They'd blast music and shimmy, shake and laugh until they could barely catch their breath. But Amy couldn't keep remembering that right now because of the promise she'd made to herself—the one about not crying any more today.

"I'm Nurse Bailey." The nurse held up her ID tag, as

though Amy might not believe her otherwise. "What's your name?"

"Amy Silverman."

The nurse swiveled to face someone else who walked into the office, which was getting uncomfortably crowded with students. "Be right with you." Then she turned back to Amy. "Good news is, your forehead doesn't look bad at all. Press this wet cloth to your head and keep pressure on it. I've got to give meds to these kids. I'll be right back to fix you up and get you on your way."

"Okay. Thanks." Amy settled onto a plastic chair in the corner. Out of habit, she tucked her right foot behind her left. Her forehead still throbbed, but more softly now. Clearly, her injury was already getting better.

Amy watched as students were given medication from little paper cups, one after the next, as if in a production line of people and pills.

While Amy waited, she observed. A good writer always paid attention to her surroundings and filtered the world around her, listening for snappy snippets of dialogue and wondering about what she saw and heard. Good writers were curious about everything and noticed small details. Amy definitely wanted to be a good writer.

"Now, let's see what's going on with that forehead of

yours." Nurse Bailey pressed the orbital bones around Amy's eyes. "Hurt?"

"Nope."

"Good. Headache? Dizziness? Blurred vision?"

"Nope. Nope. Nope."

"How many fingers am I holding up?"

"Four."

"Now?"

"Six."

"Ha ha. Seriously, how many?"

"Three."

"Right. Okay, if you get a headache or feel dizzy, or if your vision gets blurry or you see double, come back right away. We want to make sure you don't have a concussion."

Amy nodded and tried not to yip when Nurse Bailey cleaned her forehead with an antiseptic wipe and applied a bandage.

"You're good to go, Amy." Nurse Bailey nodded and then turned to another student who'd just walked in. "Marcus, how can I help you?"

Amy wanted to hear what was wrong with Marcus, because her writer's curiosity craved the rest of a story. Plus, Marcus was cute. But Amy knew she had to go. Maybe Marcus would show up as a character in one of her stories.

Amy touched the bandage on her forehead as she walked to the main office. Everyone would stare, she understood. Some people would probably ask what had happened. She decided to stick with her "walked into a door" line, if the question came up. Amy was good at creating fiction.

When she handed the teacher of her first-period class the note from the office and everyone stared at her, Amy was actually glad for the bandage on her forehead. It distracted people from noticing the heel lift at the bottom of her right sneaker as she walked to a vacant desk at the back of the room.

"As I was saying," the teacher said, "this is my favorite Jerry Spinelli novel. Perhaps it will become your favorite, too. The story takes place in Pennsylvania, not far from here." The teacher passed out copies of *Wringer*.

Amy knew she'd like this class.

She'd read Jerry Spinelli's books *Stargirl* and *Maniac Magee* and loved them, but she'd never heard of this novel. When no one was looking, Amy took a satisfying sniff of the paperback copy. It smelled like old book—her second-favorite scent. Her favorite, of course, was the crisp, inky smell of a new book. Or maybe it was her dad's blueberry waffles with warm syrup drizzled on top on a Sunday morning. Or the scent of the lavender lotion her mom used to rub on her feet after a long day of delivering mail.

Amy resisted the urge to hug the book to her chest, but she read bits of it throughout the rest of the class . . . and her next two classes.

The walk to the lunchroom after third period seemed long. In fact, Amy counted five posters that she walked past on her way—posters for a dance that had a Cinderella theme. Looking at them made the tiny hairs at the back of Amy's neck stand at attention. She'd love to go to that dance. But how? With whom? She didn't even have a friend to go with. Amy missed Kat, her friend from Chicago. She missed lots of things from back home.

Once she got her tray and trudged through the lunch line, Amy scoured the room for an empty spot at a table, but there weren't any. One table near a garbage can in the back was piled with cardboard boxes. She sat at that table, making a small space for her tray.

Amy's forehead throbbed. She thought about the boy whose shoe had hit her. Despite the circumstance, he seemed nice, in a dorky way. He'd worried that her head was bleeding and handed her that piece of paper. Amy would be okay if that boy came over to sit with her now so she wouldn't be eating lunch alone, but she didn't see him at any of the tables. Buckington

Middle was a big school, and he probably had a different lunch period.

Even though Amy filled her belly with cafeteria pizza and fries, she felt emptier and emptier as she ate. She looked down, wishing she had at least a notebook with her so she could write and create characters for company, but she'd come to school entirely unprepared. At least she had a copy of *Wringer* now. She could read.

Amy had asked her dad to buy school supplies with her, but he didn't have a chance. He promised to do it this weekend, but that would be too late. She'd have to ask Uncle Matt to take her tonight, because she needed notebooks and pens for tomorrow's classes. Of course, Amy had her special writing notebooks in a desk drawer back at the place, but they weren't for school. She needed to buy ones that were just for school.

When the never-ending day finally ended, Amy let out a big breath.

School-day tally?

Bowling-shoe-induced forehead injury: one.

Potential new friends: zero.

When Amy saw another dance poster on her way out of school, she wanted to tear it down, because if today was any indication, she wouldn't be going to that dance. She'd be like Cinderella at home *before* her fairy godmother showed up to help get her to the ball.

Too bad there aren't any fairy godmothers in real life, Amy thought. But even if there were, she was sure there wouldn't be any here in boring old Buckington.

A wisp of words whispered through Amy's mind. She almost didn't catch them.

You're right where you're supposed to be, sweets.

The Miles Spagoski Hustle

Miles was happy to be done with school and back at the bowling center, even though his dad made him clean both bathrooms and refill the toilet paper and paper towel holders before he was allowed to play.

After his chores—there were always chores!—Miles surveyed the lanes. In the third lane from the end, three guys were playing. Miles didn't recognize them. They looked like they might be in high school. That didn't intimidate him. He knew he could outplay kids of any age, as well as most adults. He put on a pair of house shoes, took a deep breath and walked over.

"Hey," Miles said to the three guys. "I was just bowling over there." He pointed vaguely toward the other end of the bowling center. "It's kind of boring bowling by myself. Mind if I join your game?"

They looked at each other; then the tallest of the guys said, "We're just starting a new game. You can play if you pay for it."

Miles tapped his chin, like he was considering it. "How many games have you already paid for?"

"We've paid through the next game," he said.

"How about I pay for the game after that?" Miles asked.

The three guys looked at each other and nodded.

"Be right back," Miles said. "Don't start without me." He jogged to the counter and quietly asked his mom to add one more game to their lane.

"Sure, sweetheart." His mom typed something into the computer. "You're all set. New friends of yours?"

"Um, sort of." Miles turned to go. "Thanks."

During their first game, Miles paid attention to how the guys bowled. They were good, but definitely not better than him. He knew he'd have no trouble beating them all in the next game. For this game, though, Miles missed easy spares and even bowled a couple of gutter balls. On purpose. It wasn't easy for him, but he had to.

After losing, Miles said, "Thanks for letting me play. Enjoy the next game." Then he started to walk away. Slowly.

The tall guy called, "Hey, you wanna play one more with us?"

Miles turned, hiding his excitement. "Um, I guess so. Sure you don't mind?"

They looked at each other and nodded.

"We could, you know, bet on this game—I mean, if you want," the tall guy said.

Miles's pulse beat wildly. Usually, he had to suggest the betting part. This was going better than he'd expected. "Um, okay." Miles pulled a ten from his pocket, hoping it wasn't too much. "Is this enough?"

The tall guy pulled out a twenty. "Was thinking something more like this." He looked at the other two guys, who yanked twenties from their pockets.

These guys were too quick to pull out their money. They kept looking at each other. Something felt off to Miles. Should he walk away? Were they trying to trick him? He glanced at his grandfather, who was sitting at the snack counter. Miles knew he needed the money to buy the gift in time for his grandpop's birthday party. "Sure, sure," Miles said, pulling the rest of the money from his pocket and pushing away the feeling in his gut that something wasn't right. "Twenty each is good."

"Then let's bowl!" the tall guy said.

"Definitely." The second guy rubbed his hands together.

"Yeah," said the third. "Let's bowl."

Miles's nerves took hold of him, and he started the

game by missing an easy spare. That would hurt him. He understood he was laying a lousy foundation. Why was he letting these guys rattle him?

The three of them bowled strikes, then more strikes. They played way better than they had in the previous game.

Miles got a sick feeling that made his legs wobbly. He'd come over to hustle these guys and earn some bank for his grandfather's gift, but now it was clear these guys were trying to hustle *him*!

Miles could distract most opponents with random chatter or weird stories about the ways people have died, but not these three. They were laser focused. Dumb tricks wouldn't work on them. Miles had to dig deep and bring his A game.

The tall guy, Kyle, bowled his third strike in a row—a turkey.

Miles's stomach tightened. How could he beat them? Miles felt like David against Goliath, except without the awesome slingshot. He couldn't even use his Blue Thunder Storm Crux ball. Miles had to bowl with a house ball so he'd look like an inexperienced player.

One important key to success is self-confidence.
An important key to self-confidence is preparation.

—ARTHUR ASHE

Bowling may be all science-y—rolling a heavy ball down a wooden lane in an effort to knock over pins—but winning . . . ah, winning . . . now, that's not science-y at all.

Often our greatest challenges come not from outside ourselves, but from within. Be careful! We can create roadblocks to our own success with the thoughts we think—the stories we tell ourselves.

What story did Bill Fong, a bowling enthusiast from Plano, Texas, tell himself the night he starting dropping strike after strike?

Mr. Fong bowled thirty-four strikes in a row during league play. Thirty-four strikes! If he'd knocked down one more pin, he would have achieved an elusive 900 series— three perfect games in a row. That coveted accomplishment has been officially recorded only thirty-two times in the United States.

Did Mr. Fong knock down that final strike at the end of the third game to complete the perfect series?

What do you think?

On the last roll of the last frame of the last game, Mr. Fong managed to knock down only nine of the ten pins. Yes, dear reader: one pin remained standing. He scored a total of 899 points.

What story do you think Mr. Fong told himself that night as he took that final roll? That he'd succeed? Or that he'd fail?

What story do YOU tell yourself when things get tough, when challenges loom large?

A "Yes, I can" story or a "No, I can't" story?

Your mind-story matters!

Are you brave enough to imagine a story—your story—with a happy ending?

Standing among these three guys who were taller and older than he was, Miles remembered some things Bubbie Louise had taught him. He remembered to follow through and bring his thumb to his nose after the shot to keep the ball straight. He remembered her telling him it wasn't about strength and speed, but about maintaining control and accuracy. *But you still have to throw the ball hard, boychik. Those pins aren't going to knock themselves down.*

Thinking of his bubbie's words, Miles reminded himself he might not be great at a lot of things, but when it came to bowling, he was the Sultan of Strikes. That was what Bubbie Louise called him when he had bowled his best game ever with her—the Sultan of Strikes!

With these thoughts swirling around in his mind, washing away negative thoughts and filling him with a tide of confidence, Miles bowled his own turkey. He followed that with a solid spare and another three strikes.

Miles told himself he could beat these guys.

Should beat these guys.

After the final frame was bowled, Miles bested the top-scoring guy by three points. Three lousy points. He had never had a game come that close when he was trying so hard to win; it made him sweat in places he didn't usually sweat. Slipping all the money off the table and into his pocket, Miles said, "Um, thanks, guys. See you later." He couldn't wait to get away from them.

"You wanna play another game?" the tall guy asked in an almost threatening way. "My treat for this one. Right?" He looked at the other two guys, who were nodding like bobblehead dolls.

But it was too late. Miles understood they were hustlers who probably hung out at Lightning Lanes over in Doylesburg but had come here to see if there were any suckers. Miles was only three points away from being that sucker, and it felt awful.

"I, um, can't. Sorry. Maybe next time."

As Miles walked away, he knew there would be no "next time"—not with those guys. To try to relax, he played video games, but it didn't work. Being repeatedly attacked by aliens was not calming. His heart beat wildly as he kept checking to see if the guys had left. He knew he wouldn't calm down until they were gone.

When they finally left, Miles joined his grandfather at the snack counter.

"Phew. That was close." Miles put his head on the counter.

"Phew what?" His grandfather took a swig from his glass. "What was close? How much did you hustle those guys for?"

Miles sat tall. "They tried to hustle *me*, Pop. Put up twenty bucks each."

"Whoa! That's a lot of dough." Grandpop Billy swirled the ice in his drink. "Must've been rich kids from Doylesburg. Kids from Buckington wouldn't have that kind of cash to bet."

"I know." Miles bit his bottom lip. "First they pretended to play badly. Then they knocked down strike after strike on the game we were betting on."

"Hmm. Sounds like how I taught you to do it."

"Exactly," Miles said. "It was terrible. I couldn't stop sweating."

Billy covered his smile with his hand. "Mm-hmm."

In that moment, telling his grandfather about how lousy it felt to almost get hustled, Miles decided he'd quit betting kids on the lanes—as soon as he had enough money to pay for Pop's big gift.

"Except for your habit of hustling kids on the lanes—which, if your parents ask, I had absolutely nothing to do with"—Billy raised his glass to his grandson—"you, Miles Spagoski, are an A-one terrific kid."

Miles looked down. He didn't feel like an A-1 terrific kid. That morning he'd said something really stupid to his best friend about their friend Tate. Then his bowling shoe had knocked some girl in the head, and she might have gotten a concussion and died, for all he knew. He might read about her someday on an online list of weird ways people have died. Finally, he'd nearly gotten hustled out of twenty bucks doing something he shouldn't have been doing in the first place.

"You are," his grandfather insisted, as though he could read Miles's mind.

"Listen to your grandfather," Stick called from his wheelchair near the billiard table. "Sometimes that old fool knows what he's talking about."

This made Miles and Grandpop Billy laugh. Stick laughed, too, as he knocked the six ball into the side pocket.

After his grandfather's seventy-fifth-birthday party, Miles decided, things would change. He'd spend all his extra time on the lanes working toward bowling that perfect game. And when he did, maybe he'd get written about in the *Buckington Times*. He knew it would make his parents and Grandpop Billy proud. Mercedes and Stick would be impressed. Maybe some random girl would find out about Miles's perfect game and want to go out with him. It could be the beginning of amazing things in his life. And it would all start right after his grandfather's big birthday party.

Thinking about it made Miles feel better than he had all day.

Heading "Home"

On her walk "home" from school, Amy realized how ridiculous she must seem, jerking her head around every so often to look out for flying bowling shoes.

Of course, there were none.

She reminded herself that the chance of getting clonked in the head with a bowling shoe twice in the same day was infinitesimal. But that wasn't really what she was afraid of or why she walked home slowly. As soon as she saw the parking lot, Amy's shoulders relaxed. There was only her uncle's car, along with a couple other cars and the hearse.

There hadn't been a funeral since Amy moved into Eternal Peace Funeral Home a week ago, and she was grateful there wasn't one today. She couldn't deal with that now, not on top of the shoe incident and her lackluster day at school. She was feeling way too vulnerable.

After entering the back door of the funeral home, Amy walked through the laundry room and into the kitchen. Even though she was allowed to enter through the front door, she didn't like going that way because it meant passing the rooms where the viewings and funerals took place.

Uncle Matt was leaning against the sink, cradling a mug. He startled when Amy walked in. "Oh, hi, Ames. How'd your first day go?"

Amy shrugged. Her uncle looked like an older version of her dad. They both had curly brown hair, but Uncle Matt had gray sprinkled throughout his, and wrinkles around his eyes. His face was clean-shaven, unlike her dad's. He was older than her dad by nine years and two days. Her dad had told her that when he and her uncle were younger, their parents would have only one birthday party for the two of them. Amy's dad used to think it was fun to share a party with his big brother, but her uncle admitted he'd been annoyed to share his party with his baby brother. Amy didn't have issues like that because she didn't have any brothers or sisters, only a dog. Well, she sort of had a dog. She looked at the picture of Ernest and Pam wearing sunglasses, then deleted it from her phone. She didn't need a reminder of what she didn't have anymore.

Uncle Matt put his mug on the counter. "Want some hot chocolate, Ames?" He put water on to boil without waiting for her answer.

"You know it," she said, trying to act cheerful.

He grabbed the packet and a bag of mini marshmallows from the pantry. "It's not hot chocolate without the—" Amy's uncle came close to her face and squinted. "What the heck happened to your head?"

"You really want to know?" Amy plopped into a chair at the small round kitchen table.

"Yes." He put the marshmallows down and sat across from her.

"I got hit by a flying bowling shoe."

"Uh-uh," Uncle Matt said. "Not one of your made-up stories. What really happened? Did someone at school do this to you? Because if—"

"I'm telling the truth. I was walking to school, and a bowling shoe hit me in the forehead." Amy had known no one would believe her.

Uncle Matt raised an eyebrow. "Come on."

"Really. I think some kids were fighting and one of them must have taken the other kid's shoe and thrown it."

Uncle Matt tugged on his earlobe, like her dad did

when he was trying to figure something out. "Why was the kid wearing bowling shoes to begin with?"

"I have no idea. But don't worry"—Amy pressed the bandage on her forehead and winced—"it barely hurts at all."

"Yeah, I can see that."

Amy didn't tell her uncle the truth about what really hurt her: Sitting with a bunch of cardboard boxes in the lunchroom at school instead of with a potential new friend. Missing her mom and her dog and her best friend. Worrying about her dad while he was away during the week, taking classes to get a license to work in the funeral home. She didn't tell anyone, but she was terrified something awful might happen to him, like what had happened to her mom. Amy knew she couldn't survive losing him, too. This last thought made her feel like a volcano about to erupt with scalding tears. But she wouldn't cry. Not now. Not in front of her uncle. "Hey, do you think we could go out and buy some school supplies?" she asked. "I need a few things for tomorrow."

"Absolutely," Uncle Matt said. "Maybe we can pick up some bowling shoe repellent while we're at the store."

Amy tried to smile, but she just didn't have it in her.

"This is why I'm a funeral director and not a comedian," Uncle Matt said as he finished preparing Amy's hot chocolate and placed the mug on the table.

"Thanks." The hot chocolate smelled sweet, and the steam tickled Amy's nose. It reminded her of sitting with her mom in their sunny yellow kitchen back in Chicago. It was getting harder and harder to hold back thoughts that Amy knew would bring on tears. She squeezed the mug until the heat from the hot chocolate burned her palms.

"We'll have to get your school supplies tonight. Can't go now. I have an appointment in . . ." Uncle Matt checked his watch. "Oh my." He rushed out of the kitchen. "School supplies after dinner," he called.

Amy felt the weight of being alone.

She sipped hesitantly but still burnt the tip of her tongue.

Hoping someone had sent her a text message, Amy pulled out her phone and felt a wave of regret for having deleted the photo of Ernest. She wished she could get it back. It was like she had erased him from her life, which she totally hadn't meant to do. Did Ernest even know how much she missed him? Did he miss her? Or had he forgotten about her? Did he curl up with Pam in bed at night like he used to do with her?

No one had texted her, so Amy sent a text to her dad.

Hi. At home. DYING to see you. Ha ha.

Her dad didn't reply. Maybe she'd pushed the humor too far.

She texted again.

Hope you're good. How's it going?

Still . . . nothing.

Dad?

Amy knew he was probably in a class, but it felt like he wasn't answering on purpose. He could at least take a break and check on how her first day at Buckington Middle went. Amy pressed the sore place on her forehead to make it hurt so it would distract from her painful thoughts.

Then she texted Kat.

Survived my first day. Barely.

Kat sent back a blue heart and three smiley face emojis.

Still in school. Text soon.

Amy put her phone back in her pocket. How had she forgotten that Chicago was an hour earlier than stupid Buckington? She took her hot chocolate and walked down the hall, past the rooms on the left she didn't want to look at. Then she turned right, toward the grand staircase with the fancy burgundy carpet on the wooden stairs. Amy unhooked the thick velvet rope that hung across the bottom of the staircase with a sign—Private Residence—rehooked the rope behind her and headed for the bedroom where she was staying.

As she climbed the stairs, her feet felt like boulders. Her forehead throbbed. Her heart was a lump of gray clay.

Amy remembered coming home from school back when her mom was feeling good—before she'd gotten sick with cancer. There would be music playing in their apartment and all the lights would be on. Her mom would give her a big squeeze and kiss the top of her head. If it was warm outside, her mom poured cranberry juice mixed with seltzer for both of them; if it was cold, she made them hot chocolate. Always with mini marshmallows and a sprinkle of cinnamon.

They'd sit together and tell each other about their day.

Whether the events of each one's day were good or bad didn't matter: it was the telling that mattered; the laughing, the listening, the being together that meant everything.

It was perfect.

It was in the past.

Past perfect.

Amy wished desperately for present perfect, but that only made her head and her heart ache.

In her room there were three things: a twin bed with worn gray quilt; a desk, next to the bed; and a nearly empty bookshelf, across from the bed. Amy kept her handful of books from home in a suitcase under the bed. There wasn't even a bureau to put her clothes in, only a plastic bin with a lid, in the closet. The room was dim and depressing. But what did she expect from a funeral home? Giant smiley faces and clown pictures in the bedrooms?

Amy placed her mug on the desk and plopped onto the bed. She fell back against the thin pillow and stared at the ceiling. Even though she'd washed the gray quilt, sheets and pillowcase, they still smelled like mold, the same way the basement in her family's apartment building in Chicago smelled. Maybe she'd ask her uncle if they could buy new bedding when they went out for school supplies.

Amy heard a woman's voice downstairs, then her uncle's warm, soothing tone, and she knew someone was meeting with Uncle Matt to plan a funeral. That must be why he'd rushed out of the kitchen.

Amy didn't know the woman, but she still felt sorry

for her. Funerals were hard. And so were the days that followed them.

. . .

There were so many people at her mom's funeral that a bunch were standing in the back and others couldn't even fit in the room. Mail carriers her mom had worked with and customers from her route came. Lots of people from her dad's Unitarian Universalist congregation came. Amy didn't know them, but they hugged her and told her how sorry they were.

Some of Amy's teachers and classmates also showed up. Even their landlord, Mr. Nadler, came. He was a nice guy. But Amy didn't want a single one of them. She wanted the person in the casket—the person who used to be her mom—to wake up and stop kidding around. Because her mom—her *mom!*—couldn't possibly be gone.

Amy didn't just want her mom back; she wanted her mom to be healthy, laughing and dancing in the kitchen with her again. She wanted her in the living room, pulling off her work shoes, putting her feet up and telling Amy about the funny things that happened on her route that day. She wanted her mom cuddling with her in bed, reading her fairy tales, saying everything would work out okay, like she did when they were at the doctor's for

Amy's leg-length discrepancy. Amy remembered how good it made her feel when her mom would say, "You'll get your happily-ever-after, sweets."

Would she ever find her way to that happily-ever-after now? Amy didn't believe it was possible without her mom.

She wanted, *needed,* her mom back. Period. End of sentence.

But that was never going to happen.

Amy held her breath and concentrated, hoping for a few whispered words from her mom to float through her mind.

Silence.

She checked her phone in case her dad had found time to text her back.

Nothing.

There was a gaping hole inside Amy that she felt would never, ever be filled.

Amy was like one of the desperate princesses from the fairy tales her mom used to read to her. Those princesses always needed rescuing by a prince, and it annoyed Amy that the female character needed a male character to save her. Girls in stories, she knew, were perfectly capable of rescuing themselves, thank you very much. And sometimes, princes needed rescuing, too.

Amy inhaled and decided she would find a way to

rescue herself from this big emptiness. She'd figure out how to rewrite the pages of her own story. There was no prince riding into the funeral home to rescue her, so she'd do it herself.

Amy would find a path to her own happily ever after.

She pulled her body off the bed that smelled like mold and found one of her writing notebooks in the desk drawer, along with her favorite purple pen that she used for creating stories.

Then Amy did the only thing she knew to craft calm from the chaos of her unpredictable life.

She wrote.

A FAIRLY HAIRY TALE

(Fiona the Fantabulous*)

BY AMY IRIS SILVERMAN

Fiona was not a princess. She was not a queen. She was not any fancy thing. Fiona was a peasant girl whose mom had died, and who had to take care of the hardscrabble farm and the ramshackle home where she lived with her aging father, Marcus, and her three-legged dog, Lucky.

Fiona, as usual, was in the field, working her way

---

* Fantabulous = Fantastic + Fabulous

through a row of purple cabbages, picking off weevils (snout beetles), minding her own peasant-y business, when a shoe came flying out of nowhere and hit her square in the forehead.

Clonk!

Seriously? A shoe!

Fiona fell to the ground, holding the bottom of her tattered apron to her forehead. It came away red. "Oh no," she groused. "Now I'll be behind in my chores because I'll have to scrub this apron in the river."

Among the beetle-infested cabbages, Fiona rose on shaky legs and spied some boys laughing and running off.

Then something shiny caught her eye.

She saw that the shoe was a lavish one. Most peasants didn't even own footwear, but this shoe had shiny black sides and a polished brass buckle on top. Fiona wondered what the brass on that buckle was worth at market. The shoe surely belonged to someone of great importance. Interestingly, when Fiona pushed her dirty foot into the shoe, it fit perfectly.

She felt a tingle radiate from her foot up to her forehead.

Then Fiona came up with a different idea, smarter than trying to sell the brass buckle at market to her neighbors, who had little more than she did and often traded food rather than coin.

With her loyal dog by her side and a few hard biscuits

in her apron pockets, Fiona decided not to wash her apron, but to find the owner of the shoe. She hoped there would be a reward for returning the lost shoe, because even a small pile of coins would make life much easier for her and her father, who had been having a hard time since Fiona's mother died. Any extra coins would help as they faced another winter with little food to share.

Shoe in hand, Fiona set off with Lucky, past the field she was so familiar with, past the small road that was rarely used, past her neighbor's puny plot of land, heading toward the town of Bumbershoot, where she'd never before been.

What would she find there? Who would greet her? Would it be safe for a peasant girl and her dog? So many things weren't safe when one wandered far from one's own village.

Most importantly to Fiona, how would she locate the owner of the mysterious flying shoe, and would she be offered any reward for her efforts?

Amy realized Uncle Matt had called her for dinner a few times before she was able to pull herself from her story and respond. "Be right down!"

Her hot chocolate had grown cold while she wrote, and her stomach growled.

When Amy placed her notebook and purple pen

on the desk and stretched her cramped fingers, she noticed a few texts on her phone.

Three from Kat.

> Hey girl.

> Hello? Where are you?

> Amy!!! Were you abducted by aliens?

Amy wrote back.

> Sorry. Was writing. Not abducted by aliens. This time. 😊

She knew Kat would understand her getting lost in writing a story, just like Amy would understand if Kat got lost in playing her saxophone. If Amy had stayed in Chicago, she and Kat would have auditioned for the arts high school together. Now Kat would audition without Amy.

There was one more text on the phone, from Amy's dad.

> Hi Pumpkin. Another looooong day of learning. Sorry to be gone during the week. Wish I'd been there for your first day of school. How'd it go? Can't wait till this weekend. Let's do something fun together. OK?

Amy was angry with her dad for hauling her to her uncle's funeral home in Buckington, Pennsylvania, where she knew no one. She was angry that her dad had to spend every Monday through Friday, for an entire month, away at some dumb training program to get certified so he could help Uncle Matt with his business, which meant they'd probably be staying in Buckington.

But the thought of spending the whole weekend with her dad, doing something fun together, melted Amy's anger.

As she headed downstairs to join Uncle Matt for dinner, she texted her dad a one-word reply:

Definitely!

She held back the rest of what she wanted to write to him—the complaining parts—because she knew if she started, she might never stop.

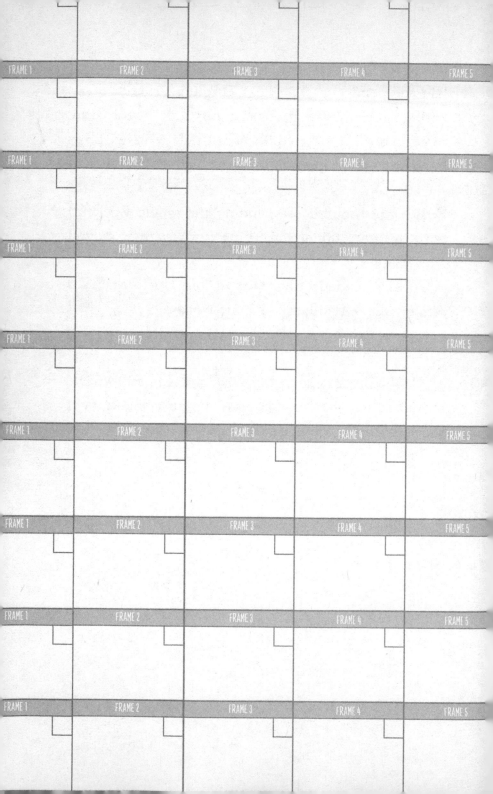

FRAME THREE

Home Is Where the Heart Is (and the Jelly Krimpets Are)

The Center of Everything

At the snack counter, Miles picked tomato wedges from his salad and dumped a heap of sour cream and chives on his steaming baked potato.

"Hey, eat those tomatoes." His dad knocked on the counter with two knuckles. "They're full of lycopene."

"Lyco . . . what?" Miles asked.

George Spagoski flipped a thin hand towel from one shoulder to the other. "It's a phytochemical, and . . . Oh, just eat 'em. They're good for you."

Miles thought sometimes his dad sounded like Bubbie Louise. She used to read science magazines for fun and would share random physics or astronomy facts, like how a two-hundred-pound person on Earth would weigh only seventy-six pounds on Mars because of the difference in gravity. And Bubbie Louise totally had a crush on astrophysicist Neil deGrasse Tyson. Miles figured if his bubbie hadn't ended up owning a bowling center, she'd have become a scientist, like Marie Curie, who won two Nobel Prizes for her studies of radioactivity. Of course, Miles found the most fascinating part of Marie Curie's life to be her death, which was ultimately caused by her exposure to the radioactive isotopes she studied.

Miles forced himself to eat one of the tomato wedges. He squeezed his eyelids tight as he swallowed the squishy lump. "Lyecopee tastes disgusting."

At the end of the counter, Miles's dad ignored him and poked at a piece of paper in front of Miles's grandfather. "Pop, we've got to make improvements around here. This place is starting to fall apart."

Grandpop Billy held up his right hand like a stop sign. "We're not changing anything, George. This place is good just the way it is." He turned to the wall where a bulletin board full of photographs hung and he addressed the center photograph. "Isn't that right, Louise?"

Miles's dad shook his head. "Mom wanted improvements, Pop. You know that. She wasn't afraid of change."

"I'm not af—" Grandpop Billy lifted his drink and slammed it onto the counter.

George Spagoski let out a breath and wiped up something that was nothing.

Miles hated when his dad and grandfather argued about the bowling center, so he tried to change the subject. "Did you guys ever hear about the French undertaker Marc Bourjade?"

"Huh?" his dad asked, looking annoyed.

His grandfather simply raised a bushy eyebrow.

"Well, glad you asked," Miles said, even though they hadn't. "Marc Bourjade, the undertaker, was in his workshop one day when a pile of caskets fell on top of him and crushed him to death."

"Ouch," Grandpop Billy said, but he was grinning.

"That's not the most interesting part," Miles told them.

"Well, what is?" his dad asked.

Miles was so excited to tell this part of the story that he accidentally popped another tomato wedge into his mouth. He grimaced and swallowed fast. "Well, it turns out Marc Bourjade was buried in one of the caskets that fell on him and killed him. Isn't that crazy—to be buried inside the thing that killed you?"

"Yeah, that's fascinating." Grandpop Billy ran a hand through his thinning gray hair.

"Where do you get this stuff, Miles?" His dad shook his head.

Miles shrugged. "Just thought it was interesting."

George turned to his father. "Dad, please consider making some changes. I have all these great ideas. We could have a weekly dance-and-bowl party on Friday nights with a DJ and one of those balls that hang from the ceiling and make rainbow light patterns. You know what I'm talking about?"

Grandpop Billy took a long, slow breath. "No dance party. No rainbow lights. No fixing things up. No changes!"

Tyler, the bowling center's mechanic, strode over. "Hey, Mr. S." He gave Miles a playful punch in the shoulder. "I'm done with all my work and the lanes are pretty empty tonight. Mind if I head out early? I promised Delilah I'd take her to the movies."

Miles swiveled around and saw that only three of the forty-eight lanes were occupied. He hadn't thought about how empty the lanes had been lately. He'd never really considered that the bowling center could be in trouble. Maybe his dad was right. Perhaps they needed to fix it up and try new things to get more people to come in.

"Go ahead, Tyler," George said. "See you tomorrow."

"Bye, Mr. Spagoski," Tyler said to Grandpop Billy. "Later, Miles." He gave Miles a fist bump and headed out.

"Dad?" George Spagoski looked at his father.

"No."

Miles's dad grabbed the papers from the counter and stormed into the kitchen.

Grandpop Billy swirled the ice in his glass and let out a long sigh.

Miles took his plates into the kitchen and rinsed them in the sink, dumping the rest of the tomato wedges into the garbage disposal before his dad could see. "I'm heading home, Dad. Thanks for dinner."

"No problem." Miles's dad shook his head. "I've got to learn not to let your grandfather get to me."

"Right?"

Miles's dad ruffled his hair. "Okay, then. I'll see you back home."

At the doorway between the kitchen and the snack counter, Miles stopped and looked at his grandfather, hunched over his drink. Miles thought about how sad his grandfather must feel without Bubbie Louise around.

His grandfather glanced up. "What're you lookin' at?"

"Nothing, Pop. I was just . . . you know, thinking about stuff."

"Well, quit thinking about stuff or you'll end up like your dad. His head's filled with too much stuff. Bunch of foolish ideas."

Miles didn't think his dad's ideas were foolish. He thought they were smart and made a lot of sense. Miles shrugged. "G'night, Pop."

Billy held out an arm, and Miles went over and let his grandfather squeeze his shoulders. "You know I love you. Right, kid?"

Miles nodded.

"Don't pay attention to anything I say. I've got a big mouth is all."

"Amen to that!" Stick called from the billiards table.

"Mind your own business," Grandpop Billy said, and squeezed Miles tighter.

Miles ducked out of his grandfather's grip. "See you back home, Pop."

Billy raised his glass.

Then Miles did the same thing he did every night before leaving the bowling center. He stood in front of the bulletin board—the one covered with photos— where a banner with big black letters read "The Greatest Stories Ever Bowled."

His bubbie Louise had created that bulletin board a long time ago to hold photographic memories of the people and events from the bowling center. There was a photo of a couple on their wedding day because their first date had been at Buckington Bowl. There was one of Miles, age three and a half, rolling a bowling ball down a purple dinosaur ramp, and a similar one of Mercedes at the same age doing the same thing. There was a photo of a woman cradling a newborn baby—a baby that was nearly born on lane 23, according to Miles's mom. She'd had to call an ambulance, and the pregnant woman barely made it to the hospital before her baby was born, three weeks early.

One photo had been on the board since the beginning.

The first photo.

The center of everything.

Miles focused on that photo—the one of Bubbie Louise when she was only twenty-two, sitting on Pop's lap. Miles's grandfather was in a wheelchair even back then. The accident had happened before he met Bubbie Louise. She looked so happy in that photo. Grandpop Billy looked impossibly young and happy, too.

Miles snuck a quick look at his grandfather now. He was still hunched over his drink, muttering to himself.

What had happened?

Death happened, Miles knew. It changed everything. Miles made sure no one was looking, then kissed his fingertips and pressed them to the photo. "G'night, Bubbie Louise," he whispered. "I still love you to the moon and back."

Miles paused, waiting for her to say the same thing to him, like she had hundreds of times before, especially when he was little.

But Bubbie Louise didn't respond.

She never would.

Death was awful like that.

. . .

Miles trudged to the front counter to grab his backpack and coat.

His mom looked up from her magazine. "Hey, Miles. Heading home already?"

He nodded.

"Don't you want to wait till we close up so we can all go home together?"

Miles shook his head. He needed quiet time to himself to think.

His mom came from behind the counter with Miles's backpack, and he let her hug and kiss him. "Everything okay, bud?"

Miles shrugged.

"Dad and Grandpop going at it again?" She nodded toward the snack counter. "Thought I heard them arguing."

"A little bit," Miles said. "I think Grandpop's still sad about Bubbie Louise."

She put a hand on Miles's shoulder. "I think Pop's sort of stuck."

"Mm-hmm." Miles felt a little stuck himself on his bubbie's being gone.

"Maybe the surprise party will snap him out of it," his mom whispered.

"Hope so." But Miles wasn't sure his grandfather was going to like a big fuss for his birthday. And he definitely worried about him having another heart attack. Surprises couldn't be good for people who've had heart attacks not too long ago. Could they? To calm his worried mind, Miles thought again about the gift he planned to give his grandfather the night of his party—the all-expenses-paid trip to Texas to visit the International Bowling Museum and Hall of Fame. Miles knew his grandpop would love the gift, especially when he found out Miles would join him and help with everything, like getting onto and off of the planes. It would be a great trip, maybe a chance to talk about Bubbie Louise so they could both start feeling better.

"Don't forget your coat." Miles's mom dashed behind the front counter and came back carrying it. "It's cold out there."

It *was* cold. Hypothermia-level cold.

Miles hurried home so he wouldn't be exposed to

the cold too long. Didn't want to take the chance of freezing to death, because that would totally ruin his chances of bowling a perfect game someday.

As soon as Miles stepped into his dark house, he felt a strange vine of anxiety creep inside him. What if some crazed killer were in the house with him? He ran straight upstairs, busted into his bedroom and turned on the light. Miles wished his family were home. He should have waited until the bowling center closed and gone home with them.

Miles took off his bowling shoes and stowed them under his bed. He was soon in his pjs and under the covers, with only small beams of light shining under his bedroom door from the hallway. That was when his mind did that thing it did when he tried to fall asleep.

First he remembered that poor French undertaker being buried under his own caskets and then inside one of them. Then his mind wandered to a dark, scary place. He remembered what his bubbie looked like in the casket at her funeral at Eternal Peace Funeral Home. Miles imagined what it would feel like to be dead and got so panicked he couldn't move. He wanted to run out of his bedroom, screaming, but literally couldn't move. It was like his body was frozen solid, but he wasn't cold. Was he actually dead? He knew he couldn't be dead, because his heart pounded like a jackhammer inside his stone-still body. Was this what death felt like, minus the beating heart?

Finally, after he heard his mom, dad and grandpop come home, Miles was able to relax. He hoped tomorrow would be a better day. Maybe during his morning matchup with Randall, he'd finally bowl a 300 game. Maybe that would be the start of a perfect day.

Or maybe . . . on his way to school, Miles would be squashed by an out-of-control Buckington bus.

Things like that could happen.

Anything could happen.

And sometimes did.

Just ask undertaker Marc Bourjade.

Not Perfect

Miles didn't roll a perfect game in the morning like he'd hoped, but he didn't hustle Randall either. That felt good.

He was glad Randall wasn't mad at him, and they seemed to be back to normal as they walked to school— Randall in his stylish sneakers and Miles wearing his lucky bowling shoes, which didn't seem very lucky at all.

So far . . .

Amy Finds a Sanctuary

During her walk to school the next day, Amy texted her friend Kat to let her know she'd decided to make one new friend today. It seemed like a reasonable goal. Amy figured there had to be one person at Buckington Middle who wanted to be her friend. If she ever wanted to create her own story's happy ending, she'd have to start somewhere. A friend seemed like the right place to begin.

Kat sent her a quick reply.

> Today will be a great day, Ames. You'll make an awesome friend and it will make everything better.

Amy texted back.

> You're an awesome friend. Thx!

That warranted a smiley face emoji and a reply:

Always knew you were smart.

Amy nodded and put her phone in her pocket. It was too cold out to keep texting.

During her first-period class, Amy smiled at everyone, thinking if she was extra friendly, people might be friendly toward her. She smiled so much, her cheek muscles ached.

A couple of kids smiled back or nodded, but mostly people ignored her. Everyone, Amy noticed, was already in a group. They'd worked out these alliances at the beginning of the school year or even before, she knew. No one was looking for a new friend in January.

No one except Amy.

In second period, she said hi to a bunch of people. Some gave half waves, but mostly they looked at her like she was weird.

Amy had taken the bandage off her forehead, but she had a small cut and yellow-brown bruising up there. She wore a heel lift in her right sneaker. She was living in a funeral home. And she preferred fictional people to real ones.

Maybe she *was* weird.

But that didn't mean she wasn't worthy of having a

friend. Back home, she had Kat. And she was friends with her neighbor Pam, who would give her all her old copies of *O, The Oprah Magazine*—Amy used to look at the photos for character ideas. Amy was friends with Elizabeth Yeh, the woman who owned their favorite bakery, the Cupcakery. She was friends with the children's librarian, Miss Irene, at her local public library. And with the guy who tended the community garden around the corner from their apartment building, Mr. Jakes.

Amy was friends with lots of people.

Back in Chicago.

During third period, no one talked to Amy except the teacher, who told her to turn in her assignment from yesterday, which she hadn't known about. She promised to have it to him by the end of the day.

On her way to lunch, Amy snuck in a quick text to Kat.

Not going well. Wish you were here.

Kat responded right away.

Wish you were here too! School isn't as much fun without you, Ames. But you've got this, Silverman!

The text gave Amy a tiny boost of confidence. She could do this. She *would* do this!

Amy bought the school lunch and sat at the end of a table with a few girls, hoping they could talk and she might learn a few things about the school. Possibly one of them would even want to be her friend. Maybe they would all want to!

As soon as Amy sat, the girls picked up their trays and went to another table. She deflated. What was wrong with her? They couldn't see the heel lift in her shoe and couldn't know she was living at a funeral home, so it must have been the dumb cut and bruise on her forehead. Or maybe the way she dressed.

Even though the girls' abandoning her had nothing to do with her mom, Amy couldn't help but think about her. That made Amy feel lonelier than ever. She looked around the crowded, noisy cafeteria and wondered how she could be surrounded by so many people and still feel so isolated.

Amy managed a few bites of her sandwich, but it was like eating layers of cardboard. Nothing on her tray had any flavor, not even the canned peach slices, which she usually loved. It was like her senses had quit working. Maybe that wasn't such a bad thing. But Amy still felt the giant, gaping hole her mom's absence had left inside her.

She dumped the rest of her lunch in the trash can,

returned the tray and made her way to the cafeteria exit. She knew she was about to cry and didn't want to do it in front of everyone.

"Where're you going?" asked a lunchroom monitor who was standing guard.

"Bathroom," Amy blurted, even though she wasn't.

"Can it wait till the bell?"

Amy shook her head but didn't make eye contact. She felt as if the dam holding back the flood of tears was about to burst.

After a pause, the woman said, "Okay. Make it quick. I don't want other kids roaming the halls, too. Who gets in trouble when that happens?"

Amy knew that was a question she wasn't expected to answer.

"I do," the woman said.

Amy nodded, then slipped past her, hoping she looked like she really needed to use the bathroom. Moving quickly, she ducked around a corner, walked down a long hallway past the bathrooms and turned another corner. There, she pressed her back and palms against the wall. Her heart thudded wildly because she was looking at a door that led outside. Amy wanted to walk through that door and never return.

Standing against the wall with her heart pounding,

Amy wondered how much it would cost to take a bus back to Chicago. Maybe she could live with Pam for a while. Then she'd have Ernest back in her life, cuddling in her lap when she got home from school. Dad said they couldn't have Ernest in the funeral home because he might disrupt a viewing with his barking. Amy knew that would be terrible, but not living with Ernest anymore was more terrible. Maybe she could move in with Kat and her family. Kat's parents always said Amy was like a second daughter to them. Then at least she'd live near Pam and be able to visit Ernest all the time.

Thoughts of moving back to Chicago made Amy feel a little better. Then a worried feeling crept in.

What about Dad? He hadn't been himself since Amy's mom died. He was quieter, and he acted like his life force had leaked out. He needed Amy. She needed him. She couldn't abandon him to move back to Chicago by herself. And she couldn't bear the idea of not having a parent in her life now. It was hard enough that her dad had to be gone weekdays for an entire month of stupid training sessions. Amy couldn't do without him all the time. She'd have to stay at Uncle Matt's funeral home, no matter how hard it was.

Amy slid down the wall a few inches and focused on some scuff marks on the floor. Her sadness slipped out in a sigh.

Then she looked up.

How had she not seen that before?

In front of her, off to the right, a word caught Amy's attention. That word was salve for her hurting heart. A single word that filled her with lightness, each letter a flicker of hope.

LIBRARY.

Amy stood tall. Her legs moved her forward. Her hand grabbed the cool handle and turned it. She opened the door and stepped inside.

The library was loaded with shelves of colorful books, banks of computers, racks of shiny magazines. Hanging on the walls were framed posters about the awesomeness of books and reading. There was a big circulation desk with a thin man pecking away at a computer keyboard.

Amy inhaled deeply, filling herself with library goodness. It smelled like . . . home.

The man behind the circulation desk looked up. "Welcome! What can I do for you?"

Amy didn't know how to answer.

The man scooted out from behind the desk. He wore a short-sleeved checkered shirt. "Hey, I don't recognize you. New here?"

Amy nodded.

His warm smile and welcoming words made Amy

feel like crying. She needed someone to be kind to her, but she wasn't prepared for how it would overwhelm her emotional circuitry.

The man offered his hand. "I'm Mr. Schu. Welcome to your library."

"Mr. Shoe?" Amy touched the sore spot on her forehead, thinking of the bowling shoe.

"Schu." He pointed to a name placard on the desk. "*S-c-h-u*. It's short for Schumaker. I'm John Schumaker, your friendly school librarian." He shook her hand with great enthusiasm.

His hand was warm. "I'm Amy Silverman."

"Hey, so come on in, Amy Silverman. What do you like to read?"

"Fairy tales." She hadn't meant to blurt it out, but something about Mr. Schu made her think it might be okay to like fairy tales even though she was in middle school. "Um, I mean—"

"Come with me, Amy." Mr. Schu led her to a section of shelves labeled Fairy Tales. There was a shelf of picture books below that. And three shelves labeled Graphic Novels to the right. *Three shelves!* Amy recognized a couple of her favorites right away—*Roller Girl* and *El Deafo*.

Her whole body tingled. She was surprised to see these books in a middle school library. Who was this guy? Had she stepped into an alternate universe? A perfect one?

"I'm new here myself," Mr. Schu said. "Started this year. I'm from Chicago."

"You're not!" Amy wondered if some fairy godmother had dropped this librarian in her path, as if a wonderful wish she didn't know she'd made had been granted.

Mr. Schu rubbed the back of his neck. "Well, actually, I'm quite sure I am."

Amy smiled. She couldn't help herself. "I'm from Chicago! Moved here last week, during winter break."

"No way," Mr. Schu said.

"Yes way," Amy replied. She realized she might be making her first friend in Buckington. Not surprisingly, it was a librarian. And a grown-up. But it was a start.

The doors to the library whooshed open. In came a group of students and, along with them, a wave of chatter.

"Uh-oh," Mr. Schu said. "I've got to set these kids up on a research project. We'll have to chat about Chicago later, Amy. For now, sit or browse. Enjoy yourself. I mean, it's a library. How could you do anything but enjoy yourself? Am I right or am I right?" Mr. Schu's smile melted the layers of ice that had formed around Amy's aching heart.

She pulled an illustrated volume titled *Cinderella* from the Fairy Tales shelf and sat on a comfortable chair at one of the tables. She ran her fingertips over the raised gold lettering on the cover and settled in to read the familiar story for what felt like the hundredth time.

Barely three pages in, Amy got the feeling she was being watched. She glanced up and saw a girl beside a cart of books. The moment Amy looked up, the girl looked down. Amy studied her because she had a sense the girl would make a great character in a story. Her clothes were an interesting combination of layered prints, stripes and solids, worn with a pair of purple Converse sneakers. And to top it all off, the girl wore a knit penguin cap over her dark-blue hair. She looked like she'd stepped off the runway of a funky fashion show.

The moment the girl turned toward Amy, Amy looked down at her book.

Who was that girl, and why was she looking at Amy? Amy felt like there was a flashing neon sign over her head: *WEIRD NEW GIRL*.

Amy forced herself to focus on the Cinderella story and soon lost herself in its pages.

"Here you go!"

Amy gasped.

The girl stood in front of her. She put down some sort of cake on a small square napkin. "Here."

"Um, what's this?" Amy asked.

As the girl hurried away, she called over her shoulder, "It's my kryptonite!"

Confused, Amy poked the spongy light-brown cake. Oil residue remained on her finger. Was Amy allowed to eat in the school library? Not at her old school, certainly. The librarian there was so mean, Amy hardly ever went in unless she had to for a school assignment.

The cake in front of Amy smelled sweet and made her mouth water. She hadn't eaten much of her lunch.

Mr. Schu was laughing with a bunch of kids at a row of computers. Even if he noticed her eating, Amy had a feeling Mr. Schu wouldn't be nasty about it. He might tell her it was against the rules, but he wouldn't make her feel bad.

So Amy stuffed a soft chunk of the cake into her mouth. It was sweet and melted on her tongue. There was a surprise inside—grape jelly filling.

"Great. Right?" the blue-haired, penguin-hatted girl asked, plopping down on the chair opposite Amy.

Amy's mouth was full. She nodded furiously.

"Jelly Krimpets from Tastykake." The girl pushed

her hair out of her eyes, but it fell right back again. "Best pseudo-food ever invented. Whatcha reading?"

Instinctively, Amy covered the book with her arm. She felt her cheeks warm.

"Don't worry," the girl said. "I read comic books and ghost stories and Jelly Krimpet boxes and—"

Amy laughed and moved her arm away. "I heard those Jelly Krimpet boxes are great reading."

"Oh, they are." The girl leaned forward. "Hmm. Okay. Cinderella's cool. It's just that she's not as kick-butt as she could be, being rescued by that dumb prince and all. And what's with those glass slippers?"

Amy subconsciously slid her sneaker with the heel lift behind her other one. Her mouth open, she stared at the girl. She'd never met anyone who shared her opinions about Cinderella before. And certainly no one who had those same opinions and sported blue hair, a knit penguin cap and a really cool combination of clothes. "I like your polish," Amy said.

The girl wiggled her fingers. "It's called Motel Pool Blue."

Amy laughed.

"So," the girl said. "Back to Cinderella. You know how at midnight everything turns back to what it was before, except for those glass slippers?"

"Yeah."

"And who the heck could wear those things? Ouch! Right? I've always wondered about that. Why couldn't she wear sneakers or something?"

Amy smiled. "I've wondered about those glass slippers, too. They seem incredibly uncomfortable."

"Finally. Someone who agrees with me. My dad says I'm being ridiculous, but I bet he's never had to wear high heels."

Amy imagined her own dad teetering in a pair of high heels and laughed.

The girl adjusted her penguin hat. "Oh, I'm Tate." She held out her hand. "Tate Elizabeth Victoria Mc-Allister."

Amy shook Tate's hand. "Amy," she said, then winced because Tate had such a strong grip. "Amy Iris Silverman."

"Sorry," Tate said. "Sometimes I forget my own strength. Nice to meet you, Amy Iris Silverman."

Then the bell for the end of the period shattered their conversation.

Amy was disappointed to have to leave Tate and Mr. Schu and the library.

"Come back tomorrow at this time, Amy, and there might be another Jelly Krimpet in it for you."

"I'll try," Amy said, but she knew she'd return to the library tomorrow even if she had to plow down the woman who stood guard at the cafeteria exit. "That sounds great."

As Amy floated out of the library into the crowded, noisy hall, her taste buds still danced with the sweet flavor from the Jelly Krimpet.

She felt light and happy through the rest of her classes. Some people even smiled at her first.

Everything was going perfectly until the final bell rang and Amy headed out into the cold, back to Eternal Peace Funeral Home.

It was at that moment Amy imagined telling her mom about her day—ached to tell her mom about her day. About meeting Mr. Schu and Tate and trying a Tastykake Jelly Krimpet. But Amy couldn't tell her mom about her day. Couldn't go home, kick off her shoes and share stories and hot chocolate with her mom. Couldn't smell the lavender lotion her mom rubbed on her feet. Couldn't dance with her mom in their little kitchen at their apartment in Chicago.

Couldn't.

Couldn't.

Couldn't.

Amy's life was filled with eternal couldn'ts.

Instead of going home to her previous perfect life, Amy had to return to a funeral home. *A funeral home!* Without her mom. Without her dad. Everything she loved was gone!

Every time Amy remembered what was missing, it felt new and horrible, like a part of her was rediscovering the pain all over again—fresh and raw. Like she had to keep remembering that her mom was gone, and along with her, every good thing in Amy's life.

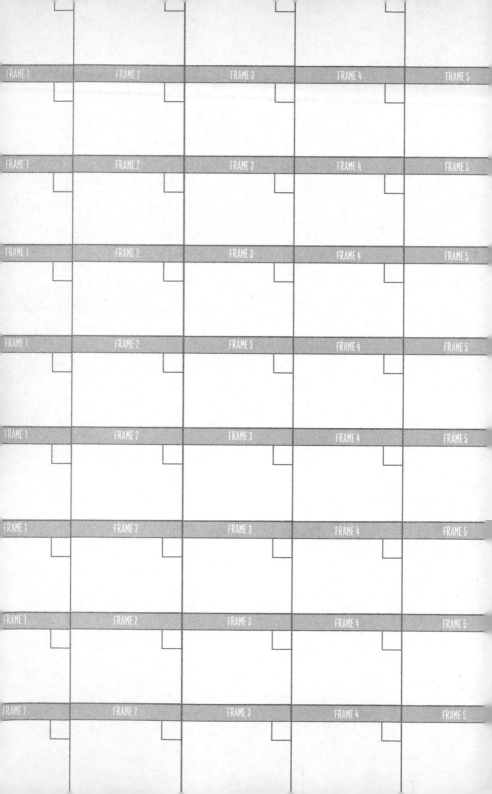

FRAME FOUR

Lost . . . and Found

Not All Those Who Wander Are Lost.

—J.R.R. Tolkien

(But Some Are)

When Amy arrived at Eternal Peace Funeral Home, the parking lot was filled to overflowing. People were dressed in fancy dark-colored clothes. Her uncle, in a suit, was helping some woman inside.

Amy's heart galloped.

She couldn't go inside.

The thing that Amy had dreaded most since arriving in Buckington was happening inside Eternal Peace right now. This would be the first funeral at the home since Amy arrived.

She. Could. Not. Go. Inside.

What if she heard people wailing/keening, and it ripped her heart to shreds? What if Amy acciden- . tally saw the dead body when she was walking past the main viewing room? What if every single part of being in the house—even upstairs in her bedroom—during a funeral reminded her of one of the most painful days of her life?

Nope.

As Amy stood outside, shivering, she wondered how her dad could choose to be involved with this. How could he want to be part of the death care industry? How could he agree to expose himself to this kind of pain on a regular basis? How could anyone?

Amy knew she couldn't. She *wouldn't*!

Even though she was practically frozen and needed to get inside somewhere warm, Amy turned back toward school. Maybe she could return to the library, where Mr. Schu would be, and she'd stay there until . . .

But the library would be closed now. Everyone would be gone. Tate would definitely be gone. Amy wished she'd thought to get Tate's number.

Not knowing what else to do, Amy turned in a different direction and put as much distance as she could between herself and the funeral home. She'd stay away for hours to make sure the funeral was over when she returned. Maybe she'd walk the 765 miles back to Chicago.

If only it weren't so cold.

Seeing all those cars, the people dressed in black, the hearse filled with flowers—all of it—triggered memories Amy didn't want to think about. Memories she tried to shove into the darkest corners of her mind.

But the memories wouldn't be forced back this time.

Memories of standing graveside as her mom's casket was about to be lowered into the ground. Her dad beside her, looking so lost, his shoulders hitching up, like he was about to crumble and land down there in the hole with her mom.

Memories of herself reaching out and slipping her fingers into her father's hand, to keep him there with her, to keep him together and solid for her. Her dad squeezing her fingers in reply. That was enough to know they'd somehow get through this. Team Silverman: now a team of two, instead of three.

She remembered the waves of people who approached her in the funeral home after the service— old ladies who were practically sweating sickly sweet perfume, telling Amy how much her mom meant to them. Amy wanted to scream that her mom meant *everything* to *her*. To Amy. She wanted every person in the funeral home to know that no one was hurting more than she was, except maybe her dad, who was hunched over on a chair with people patting his shoulders.

Amy remembered wishing it was all a nightmare,

but no matter how many times she blinked, blinked, blinked she didn't wake, so she'd had to admit it was real. She wasn't going to wake from this one. All she could do, she knew, was turn the page and hope the next one contained an inkling of happiness.

By the time Amy stopped thinking about her mom's funeral, she was lost. She'd made too many turns and hadn't been paying attention. On an unfamiliar street corner, Amy scanned the row of nearby stores: an auto parts place, a kids' consignment clothing shop, a bagel shop that was closed, a Chinese restaurant, a knitting-supply store called Knit Wits, which she thought was clever, and a UPS store, which looked a lot like USPS and reminded her of her mom again.

Amy remembered her mom in the blue uniform she wore when she delivered mail. She remembered the uniform hanging in her mom's closet when her mom had gotten too sick to keep working. And she remembered the uniform folded and placed in a box of clothing her dad gave away before they moved.

Amy sniffed.

Exhausted and numb, she leaned on a pole and sank down to the sidewalk. She pressed her back against the pole, liking how solid and strong it felt against her spine.

She thought about texting her dad but knew he

110

wouldn't be able to answer until his day of classes was over. Why did he have to start training as soon as they moved to Buckington? Didn't he realize how much she'd need him?

She thought about texting her uncle but knew he was busy coordinating the funeral for some sad family. She couldn't bother him now. Amy hoped it was the funeral of someone who was very old and had lived a good life.

She thought of texting Kat but didn't have the energy anymore.

Mostly, Amy wished she could text her mom. Talk to her mom. Hear her mom's voice. Feel the touch of her mom's hand.

Amy shivered as wind whistled and whispered around her.

What was she going to do here in Buckington without her mom or her dog or her best friend? What was she doing, living above a funeral home? How was she supposed to find her happily-ever-after with all this going against her?

Even with gloves, Amy's fingers felt like icicles. She jammed them into her coat pockets, then pulled her right hand out to swipe at her stupid leaky eyes. When she yanked her hand from her pocket, a piece of paper fluttered to the ground.

It lay there, daring the wind to blow it away.

Amy picked it up. "Oh." She almost threw it down again, but she would never litter. It was the small piece of paper Bowling Shoe Boy had given her to wipe the blood off her forehead. Now she saw that it was a coupon for a free game of bowling. Squinting at the printing on the coupon, Amy looked up at the street sign, then back down to the paper.

She was on the same street as the bowling center, a few blocks down.

Amy stood. Her legs already ached from the long walk. Her cheeks hurt from the biting wind. She decided she'd go to the bowling center, use the restroom, warm up and maybe buy a hot chocolate. Then she'd call her uncle or use the GPS on her phone to find her way back and hope the funeral was over.

Well, what are you waiting for? Her mom's voice floated into her mind, into her heart. *Go on, sweets!*

So, with a jolt of renewed spirit, Amy went.

The Unexpected

Buckington Bowl was bright and loud. Music played through the crackly speakers. Video games beeped and blipped. Pins crashed on the lanes.

It was a good kind of loud to Amy. Different from the grating noise of too many kids in the hallways at Buckington Middle, making her feel small and unwanted. This kind of loud was warm and welcoming.

"May I help you?"

Startled, Amy looked up.

The woman behind the counter closed her magazine and looked at Amy. "Did you want to bowl, sweetheart?"

Amy felt the word "sweetheart" like a thump in her chest. This woman, she knew, was probably someone's mom. *Lucky them*. Amy shook her head and walked closer. "Do you know where, um, the bathroom is?"

"I do." The woman grinned.

"Oh, I . . ."

"It's right down there, honey." She pointed toward the far end of the bowling center.

Sweetheart. Honey. Amy hadn't realized how much she missed hearing someone call her those things. "Thanks," she said, partly for the directions and partly for the woman's kindness.

Walking along the purple carpet with its bowling pins and colorful shapes, Amy took in the video games, billiard table and snack bar. It wasn't a fancy place, but it seemed comfortable. She had a feeling her mom would have liked it here.

After using the restroom, Amy climbed onto a stool at the snack counter and grabbed a sticky menu wedged between two napkin holders. She was still wearing her winter coat with her backpack over both shoulders. She didn't bother taking her backpack off because she knew she wouldn't be there long.

"What can I get for you?" asked a man with a thin towel draped over his shoulder.

Amy peered into his eyes. They looked warm, friendly. "Do you have hot chocolate?" She hadn't had a chance yet to find it on the menu.

"We do," he said.

"With marshmallows?"

"That can be arranged." The man rapped on the counter twice with his knuckles and whistled away.

Amy nodded toward an older gentleman at the other end of the counter.

He nodded back.

A boy came up and sat on the stool next to her.

"Hey, Pop," he said.

"Hey yourself," the older man replied.

Then the boy turned toward Amy, stared at her forehead and nearly fell off his stool. "You're . . . you're . . . not dead!"

"Um, of course not," Amy said, lightly touching the cut on her forehead. "Why would I be?"

"I'm so, so sorry about that. My friend Randall, he . . . the shoe . . . um . . ." The boy gulped.

Amy noted that Bowling Shoe Boy didn't seem very good with words.

The man with the towel over his shoulder put a root beer in front of the boy. "Your hot chocolate will be right up," he said to Amy.

"Thanks, Dad," the boy said.

"Dad?" Amy asked, putting the menu back between the napkin holders. She was trying to place the characters in this unexpected setting.

"Yeah," he said, sipping his root beer. "That's my dad, and my grandpop Billy is right over there."

Grandpop Billy raised his mug in greeting.

Amy gave a little wave, then held the bowling coupon in front of the boy. "So this is . . . your place?"

"Sort of. It's, um, my grandpop and bubbie's place. But she . . ." The boy nodded toward a bulletin board covered with photographs, which made no sense to Amy. "My dad and mom work here." He pointed toward the kitchen, then to the woman at the front counter.

"That's your mom?"

Bowling Shoe Boy nodded.

"She seems nice." Then Amy stuck out her hand, like Tate had done earlier in the library. "I'm Amy."

"Um, Miles." He barely touched her hand, then awkwardly dropped his hand into his lap. "Hey."

"Hi. Miles." Amy liked his name. It reminded her of Robert Frost's poem "Stopping by Woods on a Snowy Evening," which ended with these lines:

The woods are lovely, dark and deep,
But I have promises to keep,
And miles to go before I sleep,
And miles to go before I sleep.

Miles looked down and took a long slurp of root beer.

Amy cleared her throat.

Miles looked up.

Grandpop Billy chuckled. "Ah, young love." He took a swig of coffee.

Amy felt her cheeks flame. *Young love? Yeah, right!*

"Here you go." Miles's dad put a steaming mug in front of her. "Lots of marshmallows." He winked and then rapped his knuckles on the counter again.

"Thanks," Amy said, grateful for the interruption. She fished a few dollars from her pocket and placed them on the counter. Not knowing what else to do, she sipped her hot chocolate. It lived up to its name and burnt her lips.

"So." Miles let out a breath.

"So . . ." Amy wished she were home. Her real home in Chicago—with Ernest on her lap—waiting for her mom to return from work. That home. Before her mom got really sick and could barely get out of bed, much less eat anything. Amy didn't want to be sitting next to this boy whose stupid bowling shoe had cut her forehead and knocked her onto her butt, even if he was cute in a dorky way and had a name that reminded her of poetry.

"You know," Miles said, "your forehead doesn't look nearly as bad as I thought it would."

"Um, okay." Amy sipped her hot chocolate again. Even though it was still quite warm, she wanted to finish it and get out of there. Why had she even come?

"I'm just glad you're okay." Miles took another long slurp of soda.

Amy nodded. She understood that Miles couldn't know how far from okay she felt on the inside.

"Want something to, um, eat?" he asked.

Amy shook her head, even though she was hungry.

"We've got some really good desserts." Miles yanked the sticky menu from between the napkin holders. But he pulled too hard, because the menu knocked into his glass of root beer, making it teeter at the edge of the counter like a bowling pin about to . . .

TOPPLE OVER!

The icy contents of Miles's glass spilled, splashed, sloshed onto Amy's lap like an Arctic wave.

Amy jumped off the stool. "Oh!"

"Sorry! Sorry!" Miles grabbed a bunch of tiny, flimsy napkins from the dispenser and wiped at Amy's legs, depositing shreds of paper on her jeans.

"Stop!" Amy shrieked.

Miles stopped.

Amy turned and fled, leaving the marshmallows to

melt in her abandoned hot chocolate. As she ran, her sneaker with the heel lift slipped off. She had to stop and pull it back on. Then, without glancing behind her, Amy sprinted through the doors and away from the bowling center faster than Cinderella ran from the ball when the clock struck midnight.

No Redemption

The only sound Miles heard above the clatter of pins on the lanes and oldies music piped through crackly speakers was coming from Grandpop Billy. He was laughing so hard his shoulders bobbed like a silent jackhammer.

"It was an accident!" Miles screamed as he ran through the automatic doors and into the parking lot, forgetting to put on his coat. Could someone die of hypothermia from standing in a bowling center parking lot in January for only a few minutes? Probably!

It didn't matter. Miles had to tell Amy how sorry he was. Had to make her understand he wasn't usually so clumsy. If only she could see him bowl. Miles looked around desperately, past his parents' orange van, past

the half-dozen cars in the lot, hoping for a glimpse of Amy.

Miles shivered mightily.

It was too late.

She was gone.

Miles knew there was nothing he could do to fix this now, so he trudged back inside, rubbing his hands together to warm them, and helped clean up the mess he'd made.

A Precarious Place to Be

Amy ran down to the block that had the stores and restaurants. There, she caught her breath and put the funeral home address into her GPS. She felt like Hansel and Gretel following bread crumbs through the forest as she followed the walking directions on her phone.

Amy walked slowly—so slowly—afraid the funeral might not be over yet. The wet root beer on the front of her pants turned icy cold. She was sure she'd have frostbite on her legs thanks to that boy. How did he manage to knock his entire soda over onto her lap?

Amy thought she should probably avoid Miles in the future. He was dangerous!

If she walked any slower right now, she'd be going

in reverse. She didn't want to get back to Eternal Peace, even though it was dark outside and so cold. She didn't want to walk in on someone's funeral. Why had her dad moved her there? Couldn't he have found another good job somewhere else? Couldn't he have—

Amy stopped.

She texted her dad.

Thinking of you. Hope you're having a good day.

When her dad didn't respond, she texted Kat a tiny lie.

The day was a little better. How are you?

Kat didn't answer either.

Amy stood there on the street, checking her phone every few seconds even though it hadn't vibrated. When she got so cold she couldn't stand it, she forced her legs to move forward.

Back at Eternal Peace, the parking lot was practically empty.

That meant the funeral was over.

Amy had stayed out long enough.

She opened the front door with stiff, aching fingers. She was too cold to walk all the way around to the back door.

Inside the house, Uncle Matt and a couple other people were cleaning up the room where people went to eat and have coffee and talk about the person who had passed. Uncle Matt and the others were taking white cloths off the tables and sweeping the floor. Amy knew she should offer to help, but she couldn't. Not now. Instead, she tiptoed past the velvet rope and went upstairs.

After taking a long, warm shower and changing into dry pants and a sweater, Amy went to the kitchen and made mac and cheese and broccoli for herself and Uncle Matt. They had mini peach pies for dessert. Then Amy went to her room.

She texted her dad again.

How's it going?

She pulled out her notebook and purple pen, but her dad responded right away.

You have no idea how exhausting all this is.
Is it the weekend yet?

Amy texted back.

Two more days. You can do it!

Even though she didn't feel it, Amy tried to be upbeat in her texts to her dad.

She smiled and tapped her phone to reply: 😊

What she really wanted to reply with was 😟. And maybe even the poop emoji.

She wanted to crawl under the moldy-smelling quilt and sleep until it was the weekend and her dad came home and made everything better. But Amy knew that before she went to sleep, she had to write. It was a compulsion that had gotten worse since her mom died.

So Amy did the one thing she knew how to do well—she returned to writing her story. She'd had ideas throughout the day that she had to get down before she lost them to the ether. Amy thought about how many perfectly good ideas were probably floating around in the universe because people didn't take time to capture them by writing them down. She wouldn't let that happen to hers. She wasn't willing to lose another thing, even the scrap of a story idea.

It took Fiona and her dog, Lucky, until dark to get to the town of Bumbershoot.

Once there, Fiona realized how hard it would be to find the person the shoe belonged to. Why hadn't she given enough thought to that before she embarked on this journey? She had been distracted by thoughts of receiving a reward. She knew she'd have to look for someone wealthy enough to own a shoe that fancy. But how would she—a peasant girl—be received at a place of worth?

Fiona pulled her shoulders back, trying to make herself feel worthwhile, like she belonged in any place of high regard, even though a tiny voice inside her told her she didn't.

Fiona came across fields that didn't look so different from the fields where she lived back home. But these fields felt different, especially because it was nighttime and Fiona was never out in her fields at night. Darkness was a time for sleeping, not for tromping through the outdoors. In fact, Fiona felt awfully tired. But she was scared, too, which kept her mind alert.

She hadn't expected to miss her father, but she did. Desperately. And Fiona realized she hadn't told him where she was going or why. He would surely worry for her safety.

Should she simply return home? Abandon her quest?

It would be such a long walk back. And if she gave up on getting a reward for the shoe, they'd remain in the same sad situation—winter coming and not enough food. Never enough food!

"What do you think?" Fiona whispered to her loyal dog.

Lucky looked up at her with big, hopeful eyes and barked once.

"Shush. No telling who's out here with us." Then Fiona gave him a few pieces of her hard biscuit because he was such a good dog, and she knew he must be as hungry as she. At the sight of the biscuit, Fiona's stomach erupted with a growl nearly as loud as Lucky's bark. She quieted her belly with a few pieces of biscuit for herself. "That's it for now," Fiona told Lucky. "We've got to make it last. Let's go find something to drink and, I hope, the person to whom this shoe belongs. I'm sure he'll want it back."

Even though her legs were weary and she was thirsty and afraid, Fiona soldiered on. She and Lucky tromped through dark fields and crossed dirt roads until they came upon a massive structure—bigger than anything Fiona had ever seen.

It was an enormous stone castle, surrounded by a moat that burbled below the grassy bank under Fiona's feet. The night was dark, with barely a quarter moon to light their way, and she could see no way to cross the moat. Fiona was glad for the dim light because she didn't want to see what creatures lived in the moat—those she imagined were frightening enough. And she didn't want anyone to be able to see her and Lucky either.

A creaking sound broke through the night. Chains were released as a heavy drawbridge was lowered from the castle until it thumped hard onto the bank next to Fiona and Lucky.

The vibrations made Fiona shudder.

Lucky backed away from the edge of the drawbridge and tucked his tail between his legs.

"It's okay, boy," Fiona whispered, reaching down to pet the top of her dog's head, even though she wasn't sure anything was okay.

A hulking, shadowy figure appeared from the castle and marched toward Fiona and Lucky.

"Maybe we should go home." Fiona wished she could sprout wings and fly all the way back home with Lucky secure in her arms. But the truth was, Fiona couldn't move. Her legs felt like solid tree trunks with long roots planted firmly in the ground.

As the figure advanced, Lucky growled but moved back another few steps.

Fiona wished desperately she were home, sleeping in their humble abode, with her father on his bed of straw, snoring wildly. Not having enough food to last through winter didn't seem so bad at the moment. She wondered why she'd made the long, dangerous journey and silently cursed the shoe that had brought her there, the one clutched in her trembling hand.

Fiona smelled the figure before she saw him clearly. He stank of sweat and old meat. And blood. He smelled like . . . trouble.

The huge man planted his dirt-encrusted boots and held a spear across his chest. "Who goes there?" he demanded. "What business have you with the royal family?"

Lucky shivered beside Fiona's leg.

Fiona shook, too. She held out the shoe with its shiny buckle, which seemed dull in the weak moonlight. "I—I . . . found . . . ," Fiona stammered, her heart a clenched fist.

"Speak, girl!" the huge man demanded.

How had she gotten herself and Lucky into this mess? At least, she consoled herself, it couldn't possibly get worse than it was at this miserable moment.

That was when many more men, bigger and broader than the first, came pounding, thumping, pulsing along the drawbridge toward them, spears and spirits raised. "Aaaiiiiiyyyaaa!"

A vibration from Amy's phone startled her. She didn't want to leave her story world, didn't want to abandon Fiona and Lucky in danger, but the text was from Kat, so Amy reluctantly let the story world slip away and focused on her phone and the real world.

I'm so glad you made a friend today.

Thoughts of Tate flooded Amy's mind. Tate's Motel Pool Blue nail polish. The Jelly Krimpet. The penguin hat. Her tight grip when she shook Amy's hand. And

129

the crazy combination of clothing patterns she wore that somehow looked really cool on her.

Amy texted:

She'll never be as awesome as you.

Kat's response was quick.

Course not!

Amy sent a few silly emojis.
Then Kat wrote:

Tomorrow will be even better for you.
Btw Mom said I could visit in the spring.

Awesome!!! Sneak Ernest into your suitcase.

Wish I could!

Amy put her notebook and pen away. She realized how tired she was.

There's this boy, she texted.

Yes???????????

He spilled his drink on me.

No!!!!!! Smooth move, Romeo.

I know. Right?

Stay away from that one.

If Amy had been honest, she would have admitted there was something about Miles she didn't want to stay away from. Something in his eyes. Something about the way he'd said "Sorry. Sorry." Like he'd meant it. Something charming about his impossible klutziness.

I will, I guess.

But would she?

Whatcha doing now?

Going to bed.

What? It's so early!

It's 11:30!

Forgot. It's 10:30 here.

Oh, right. G'night, Kat.

G'night, Ames. 🐟🐣🐹🐥🐱🐴💀🐼 zzZ zzZ zzZ

As Amy drifted off to sleep that night, gentle words from her mom floated through her mind: *G'night, sweets. Pleasant dreams.*

Amy sighed and settled in. *G'night, Mom. I love you. Love you, too, sweets.*

Determination

Miles woke with a dreadful, heart-pounding feeling, like something terrible might happen. Maybe he'd just had a bad dream. Whatever it was, he felt exhausted and wished he could go back to sleep. But if he hoped to get in a few practice frames before Randall arrived at the bowling center, he had to get moving.

As Miles dressed, he remembered spilling his root beer all over Amy's lap. Great way to make up with her for what happened to her forehead. Why was he such a klutz sometimes?

Miles knew bowling would take his mind off what a fool he'd made of himself with Amy. The bowling center was the one place he felt confident he'd have all the right moves, where at least he knew what the right moves were. Where everything made sense, and he was too practiced to make a fool of himself or do anything clumsy. Where it felt easy to be his best self.

Miles got to the bowling center before Randall, and the extra bit of practice paid off. He beat Randall by thirty-eight points and snapped up a cool five bucks from his friend, reminding himself that when he had enough for his grandfather's gift—which he almost did—he'd be done betting people on the lanes. Miles remembered how it made him feel when those guys nearly hustled him.

Randall tied the laces on his shiny sneakers. "I'm asking her today."

"Asking who?" Miles switched from one pair of bowling shoes to the other.

Randall hit Miles in the chest with the back of his hand. "Tate. The dance. Duh."

"Oh, yeah." Miles avoided thinking about the dance, even though there were posters everywhere at school and people kept making more and more elaborate dance-posals. "How are you going to ask?"

"I have a sign and . . . there's this thing I need to . . . well . . . you need to help me."

"Oh, *great*."

Randall stood and shrugged on his jacket. "Thanks for all the support."

"Sorry. Sorry. I'll help. What do I have to do?" Miles ran his fingers through his hair. "Can't you just, you know, ask her? You've been friends for, like, forever."

"No, I can't just ask her! Come on. I'll tell you everything on the way to school. I don't want to be late."

Miles took a breath. "For the ten-billionth time, Rand, we're not going to be late."

As the boys grabbed their stuff, Grandpop Billy called from the snack counter, "Hurry up, you two, before you're late!"

"Told you," Randall said.

Miles looked over at his grandfather, about to tell him they weren't going to be late. But his grandpop's face seemed pale. Paler than usual. Maybe it was the dim lighting over the snack bar, but something didn't seem right, and Miles had had that worried feeling when he woke today. "You need anything before we go, Pop?"

Grandpop Billy waved them away, then put his hand on his chest. "I'm good. You get going now."

Why did he put his hand on his chest like that? Miles wondered. *Is he getting pains again?*

"Let's go!" Randall insisted, pulling on Miles's sleeve.

The boys hurried to the doors of the bowling center with Miles glancing back at his grandfather. *Please be okay, Pop.*

Miles and Randall left the warmth of Buckington Bowl to face the frozen tundra on their walk to school. The whole way, while Randall explained his plan to ask Tate to the dance, Miles worried that his grandfather might have another heart attack. And this one, he feared, could be worse than the last.

During first period, Miles thought he'd explode from worry, so he got a pass to go to the bathroom, and he texted his mom from there.

> Pop didn't look good this morning. He was holding his chest, like maybe it hurt. Let me know he's okay. Okay?

His mom replied right away.

> Your grandpop's fine, Miles. I'm right here with him, having coffee. Stop worrying!!!

Miles was sure that his grandpop's face had looked extra pale that morning, and that he'd put a hand on his chest like something was wrong.

So even though his mom texted that his grandpop was fine, Miles kept worrying.

It was the one thing, besides bowling, he was good at.

FRAME 1	FRAME 2	FRAME 3	FRAME 4	FRAME 5

FRAME 1	FRAME 2	FRAME 3	FRAME 4	FRAME 5

FRAME 1	FRAME 2	FRAME 3	FRAME 4	FRAME 5

FRAME 1	FRAME 2	FRAME 3	FRAME 4	FRAME 5

FRAME 1	FRAME 2	FRAME 3	FRAME 4	FRAME 5

FRAME 1	FRAME 2	FRAME 3	FRAME 4	FRAME 5

FRAME 1	FRAME 2	FRAME 3	FRAME 4	FRAME 5

FRAME 1	FRAME 2	FRAME 3	FRAME 4	FRAME 5

FRAME FIVE

Forward Motion

It's Official

Thursday morning, when Amy and her uncle were eating oatmeal together at the kitchen table, Uncle Matt ran a hand over his face. When he looked at Amy, she noticed dark semicircles underneath his eyes, like tiny dark half-moons.

"I'll be glad when your dad finishes his training and can help me around here," Uncle Matt said. "I need another set of well-trained hands. With his background, your dad will be a great asset."

Amy took her bowl to the sink and rinsed it. She knew her uncle meant that her dad had been a wonderful minister for the Unitarian Universalist church back in Chicago. He had helped a lot of people from the congregation. He was good at it. But when Amy's mom got sick, he left his position at the church and spent several months taking care of her. Once her mom died, the church had already replaced her dad with another minister. Amy understood the church's leaders couldn't wait around forever, but she didn't like it. If her dad could have gone back to the church, they'd probably still be living in Chicago.

"I'd better start working," Uncle Matt said. "Lots to do today."

Amy gave her uncle a hug. "Hope you have a good day."

"You're the best." Uncle Matt took Amy's hand and squeezed. "I'm glad you're here, Ames."

As she walked to school, Amy thought about what her uncle had said, that he was glad she was there. She hadn't thought of that. Maybe Uncle Matt needed some family around. Maybe this move wasn't all about her.

At lunch, when Amy tried to leave the cafeteria, the same woman stood guard. "Where do you think you're going?"

Without hesitation, Amy said, "Library aide."

"Next time, get a pass or I won't be able to let you go." The woman narrowed her eyes at Amy.

"Absolutely."

Amy suppressed an urge to run to the library,

because she didn't want to get in trouble. There might be a Jelly Krimpet waiting for her, she knew. And a potential new friend.

"Hey there, Amy Silverman from Chicago," Mr. Schu said when she opened the door to the library.

"Hi!" Amy said, feeling instantly lighter.

Across the library, she saw Tate's blue hair, tucked under her knitted penguin hat. And a new wild combination of clothes. Amy waved like she'd spotted an old friend.

Tate motioned her back to a table near the fairy-tale collection.

Amy rushed over and sat at the table with Tate.

Tate pulled out Jelly Krimpets in plastic wrappers—one for each of them. "Did I tell you my best friend moved away right before school started?"

Amy shook her head and thought of Kat. She knew what it felt like to lose a best friend because of a move.

"Yup," Tate said. "Her mom's in the military, and they moved overseas, which totally stinks. Perla and I were going to start a fashion blog, and we always did our consignment store shopping together on weekends."

"Oh."

Tate picked at the plastic wrapper in her hand. "She liked the Butterscotch Krimpets best."

Amy didn't know what to say because she'd never eaten a Butterscotch Krimpet so she nodded.

"But the jelly ones are the best kind." Tate looked at Amy. "I'm glad you came back to the library today, Amy Iris Silverman."

Amy thought of how alone she felt in the sea of people in the cafeteria. "Me too." Looking at Tate, Amy realized maybe she wasn't the only one who needed a friend. "I wish I could come to the library every day at lunch."

Tate ripped open the wrapper, shoved an entire Jelly Krimpet in her mouth and spoke around it. "You can."

Amy tilted her head.

"Come with me." Tate grabbed Amy's wrist and pulled her to the circulation desk. "Mr. Schu," Tate said, her mouth still stuffed, "Amy wants to be a library volunteer."

Mr. Schu put aside the book he was holding. His face looked very serious. "Well, Amy Silverman from Chicago, what are your qualifications for the exalted position of Buckington Middle School Library Aide?"

"Well, I, um—"

"Just kidding," Mr. Schu said. "I can tell you're a book lover of the highest order." He gently touched the top of Amy's head with the book he'd been holding. "I officially dub you a library aide." He handed

Amy a laminated pass—a key to the kingdom. "Show this to the lunchroom sentry. You're welcome to come here every day during your lunch period. I'll be happy to have your help."

Amy held the pass to her chest like she would a new book. "Thank you."

"Thank you!" Mr. Schu came out from behind the desk, pushing a cart filled with books. "Now that it's official, here's a bunch of books to shelve. We can always use an extra set of hands around here, especially hands that understand the power and magic of books."

Amy did understand those things. And she loved being around other people who understood them. It was like belonging to a secret society.

Tate helped Amy pull the cart over to the shelves and showed her how to figure out where the books belonged based on the label on their spine. Once Amy got the hang of it, the two chatted quietly about books, boys, Jelly Krimpets and Tate's love of weight lifting, while students came into and went out of the library.

Amy and Tate looked up at the same time when two particular boys walked in.

One was dressed stylishly, with shiny new sneakers; the other was wearing bowling shoes.

The Asking

"Hello there, Miles Spagoski and Randall Fleming."
Mr. Schu gave each of the boys a fist bump as the two
of them walked past his desk.

Amy wondered if Mr. Schu already knew the name
of every student in the entire school.

The boys walked over to where Amy and Tate were
shelving books. Miles was carrying a backpack.

"Randall has something to tell you," Miles announced to Tate. He nodded at Amy.

Tate stepped forward, hands on hips. "Then Randall can say it."

Randall took a step backward.

Miles leaned toward Amy and spoke quietly. "By
the way, I'm really sorry about spoiling, um, spilling
my soda on you yesterday."

"Me too." Amy shook her head. "I mean . . . it's okay."

Miles's half smile got Amy's attention. It made him look adorable. Or maybe adorkable. She wasn't sure which.

"*Miles* was the one who spilled the soda on you?" Tate busted out laughing.

Amy's face flamed red. She wished she hadn't just told Tate about the embarrassing incident.

Miles's face, Amy noticed, looked even redder than hers felt. This made him seem even more adorable. What was wrong with her? This boy's bowling shoe hit her in the forehead and he spilled soda all over her lap. Why was she feeling so tingly being near him?

While Amy wondered about this, Randall dropped onto one knee in front of Tate. For a moment, Amy thought Randall might be hurt and she should yell to Mr. Schu for help.

"Tate?" Randall asked in a whisper-wobbly voice.

Tate chomped on another Jelly Krimpet. "Yeah?"

"Okay, here goes. . . . Tate Elizabeth Victoria Mc-Allister, I couldn't *weight* to ask you to the dance."

At that, Miles pulled a ten-pound hand weight from the backpack and did a bunch of arm curls.

Mr. Schu and the other kids in the library gathered around to watch.

Randall cleared his throat. "It would be really *sweet* if you'd go with me."

After that cue, Miles reached into the backpack, pulled out an entire cardboard box of Jelly Krimpets and handed them to Tate.

Tate staggered backward as though someone had pushed her.

The kids standing around laughed.

Tate touched her fingertips to her chest. "You want to go to the dance . . . with me?"

Randall, still on one knee, nodded so hard, Amy thought his teeth might clack together.

Tate blinked a few times. "Well then, Randall Fleming the Third, heck yes!"

Amy felt her eyes fill up. This was more romantic than the best fairy-tale love story she'd ever read. She could barely keep herself from jumping up and down and clapping.

Randall let himself fall backward and collapse, a hand over his heart. A laugh burst from his lips, but that quickly turned into a cough. Randall was lying on the floor, coughing.

Amy saw Miles's eyes grow wide. "You okay?" she asked him gently.

Miles shook his head. "Huh?"

Amy touched his shoulder. "Miles?"

Randall sat up and cleared his throat. "Phew, that wasn't so bad."

Miles let out a quick breath. "Okay. He's okay."

Amy wondered why Miles got upset that Randall was goofing around.

Tate was beaming.

Mr. Schu and the kids standing around applauded, then went back to what they'd been doing before the big dance-posal.

Amy wondered if Miles might get down on one knee now and ask *her* to the dance. But she realized that was a ridiculous fantasy. After all, she didn't know much about the boy, other than that he wore bowling shoes to school and was kind of clumsy, which would probably make him an awkward dancer anyway.

Tate giggled, and Amy pulled herself back to what was actually happening and how happy Tate must be. Good feelings bubbled up, and a smile spread across Amy's face. She couldn't help it, because it felt so good to be included in this moment.

Miles offered Randall a hand and pulled him up from the floor.

Randall moved in to give Tate a hug and seal the deal.

Tate, much shorter than Randall, grabbed him around the middle and lifted him off his feet.

All four of them cracked up.

"Well, I guess I'll see you later, then," Randall said, nodding at Tate.

"Definitely," Tate replied. "I mean, you live next door to me."

"Oh, yeah." Randall ducked his head. "That's true."

"See you," Miles said, looking at Amy.

Amy felt a shiver run from her forehead to her feet. She offered Miles a little wave and a shy smile.

Mr. Schu gave Randall a double thumbs-up when the boys passed the circulation desk.

Tate and Amy went back to shelving books, but they got very little work done between talking and giggling about what had just happened.

"Randall's got piles of brothers and sisters," Tate told Amy. "I always love the noise and commotion when I go over to his house." She looked down for a moment. "And I've had a crush on that boy since we were in third grade and he used to wear a bow tie to school."

"A bow tie?" Amy asked.

Tate nodded. "And look at him now. That boy is the only one in this whole boring school with any style." Tate twirled, her checkered skirt flaring out. "I mean, besides me."

Amy thought Miles had a style, too, with those

bowling shoes he wore. It was just that Miles's style was . . . different.

"Would you help me pick out a fun outfit to wear to the dance?" Tate asked. "And shoes? I mostly have different-colored and -patterned Converse sneakers. I know if Perla were still here, she'd have gone with me to the consignment shops, but . . ."

Amy felt like Cinderella—being asked to help Tate find something to wear to the dance, but not going to the dance herself. "Sure," she said. "That would be fun." She was glad to be asked. "But Converse might be a fun footwear choice for the dance."

Tate tilted her head. "You might be right. Hey, want to come over after school today and we can talk more about it? I'll text my parents and let them know."

"Yes!" Amy said too loudly. Then, more softly: "I'll let my uncle know."

"Awesome sauce!"

Amy appreciated that Tate didn't ask why she'd let her uncle know instead of, say, her mom.

The two girls high-fived hard.

Amy's hand stung a little, but she didn't mind.

She was feeling pretty good when the bell rang and Tate gave her an extra Jelly Krimpet. "I'll meet you outside the library after school, and we'll walk to my house together. Okay?"

"Definitely!"

Mr. Schu nodded at Amy as she walked past his desk. And that nod made Amy feel wonderful, like he knew, too, that things were finally turning around for her.

Imagination is more important than knowledge. Knowledge is limited, whereas imagination embraces the entire world, stimulating progress, giving birth to evolution. —ALBERT EINSTEIN

Mr. Schu nodded, because he knew magic could happen in the library—all kinds of magic, not just book magic. And he was like the magician who helped it happen. Libraries and good librarians are wonder-filled like that. If you don't believe me, it's probably because you haven't discovered a magical library or librarian . . . yet.

I hope you do, though. They can make a life-changing difference. You just don't always realize it at the time. Libraries can help you fall in love with science or travel or math or . . . ideas. Libraries house a collection of the thoughts, ideas and imagination from so many people across so many times. Quite a wondrous thing, if you stop and think about it.

But for now, let's think about Amy and Miles and the story at hand.

We're approaching the especially good parts. You don't want to miss anything important, like Marmalade. She may be only a cat, but she matters . . . as do all Earth's creatures.

Oh, you'll see what I mean.

Enough with this paws, er, pause in the story.

Onward!

Dead and Breakfast

Tate's house, it turned out, wasn't a house. It was the Buckington Bed & Breakfast, established in 1987. There was a sign out front, on a black iron frame, that for some reason Amy read as *Buckington Dead & Breakfast, est. 1987.* She wondered for a moment what it would be like to combine a bed-and-breakfast with a funeral home. That would certainly be the ideal name for it, but she couldn't imagine anyone wanting to stay there. Amy shook the thought from her head, because it was weird. *She* was weird. But she did think a B and B funeral home might make an interesting setting for a story someday.

Tate clapped her mittened hands together. Her nose was bright pink. "I'm so glad you could come over today."

"Me too," Amy said, and she was, because it was nice not to go back to the funeral home, to the likelihood of a viewing taking place. She didn't say this to Tate.

Inside Buckington Bed & Breakfast, there was a wooden desk where guests checked in, and beyond that a small dining room with big windows, a living room with a grand piano and shelves that were loaded with books and board games, and a set of stairs that, Tate explained, led to their six guest rooms.

Buckington Bed & Breakfast was much more cheerful-looking, Amy noted, than Eternal Peace Funeral Home, with its somber colors and old-fashioned furniture.

Amy shivered with happiness at being there.

A calico cat slunk into the room and rubbed against Amy's right ankle.

Tate scooped up the cat and petted behind her ears. "Who's a good girl?"

"So Randall lives near you?" Amy asked.

"Right next door." Tate cradled her cat. "But I end up going over there instead of him coming here, because he's allergic to Marmalade."

Amy looked into the dining room. "He's allergic to marmalade? Like jam?"

Tate laughed and held up her cat. "This is Marmalade."

"Oh."

"Want to hold her?"

Amy wasn't sure, but she accepted the cat carefully. Marmalade nuzzled into her neck and purred. It reminded her of coming home to Ernest and how good that always made her feel. She didn't want to let go of the warm, soft cat.

"Wait here!" Tate ran off. She returned with an instant camera—the kind that takes pictures and prints them right away. Tate took a photo of Amy cuddling with Marmalade and handed it to her while gently taking the cat from her arms. "Let's go to my room."

Tate put Marmalade on the floor, and the cat darted upstairs.

"What a sweetie." Amy followed Tate while keeping an eye on the developing photo.

"She's really friendly with the guests. They write nice things about her in their online reviews."

Amy imagined what people might write about Ernest in an online review. That he had big, sweet eyes. That he always begged for food. That he knew when you needed him most and would curl up in your lap anytime, no questions asked.

The walls of Tate's bedroom were covered with posters of female bodybuilders, some of whom were lifting barbells that looked impossibly heavy.

When Tate took off her coat, Amy noticed how

muscular her arms were. She remembered Tate hoisting Randall off his feet and how Tate had practically crushed Amy's hand the other day when she shook it. "So you love weight lifting?"

"Oh yeah. I go to the gym every other morning with my dad before school. He's my coach. I just started competing."

"That's so cool." Amy tucked this little fact into her mental writer's notebook. She knew it would make an interesting detail for a character in one of her stories someday.

Tate flexed a bicep, and Amy could see, even underneath Tate's sleeve, how large and defined her muscle was.

"Remind me not to get you mad at me," Amy said.

Tate plopped onto her bed and pointed to a chair for Amy to sit on. "No worries there. I can't imagine getting mad at you. Besides, I use my powers only for good—you know, winning competitions."

Amy took off her coat and hung it over the back of the chair. She sat, still holding the photo, which was almost fully developed. "How'd you get into weight lifting?"

"It's just something I started doing when I joined my dad at the gym one day and realized how much I liked it."

Amy felt that way about writing. She wrote a story

one day when she was bored and hadn't been able to stop writing since.

When the photo showed clearly, Amy passed it to Tate. "Marmalade's a*dor*able."

"Thanks." Tate tapped the photo. "Randall's so allergic to cats, he'd probably start wheezing from looking at this." She passed it back to Amy. "Keep it."

Amy tucked the photo into her coat pocket. "Thanks."

Near Tate's bed, in a wicker basket, were balls of colorful yarn. Tate pulled out two knitting needles and some purple yarn and began moving her fingers fast. "Do you want a snack or something?"

Amy shook her head, mesmerized by what Tate was doing. She noticed there were knit animal hats on surfaces all over the bedroom: A koala. A monkey. Two zebras. And an elephant. "You made all these?"

"Yup." Tate's fingers never stopped moving, knitting needles clack, clack, clacking. "I sell them through my online store, Hats Off to You."

"Oh my gosh. I love it."

"Thanks. It's something my aunt Annette taught me to do a few years ago. Do you knit?"

Amy shook her head.

"Want to learn?"

"Um, I guess so."

Tate showed Amy how to do a simple stitch with some multicolored yarn that had a Knit Wits label on it.

After a couple hours' effort, Amy had knit half a crooked square. She felt quite proud of herself.

In that same time, Tate had made an elephant hat and held it up for Amy to admire before putting it into a padded envelope to mail to a customer. "Custom order," she said. "They wanted a purple elephant. I think it looks pretty cool. You like?"

"It's amazing." Amy bit her lip. "Hey, thanks for inviting me over. I'm really glad I met you, Tate Elizabeth Victoria McAllister."

Tate ducked her head. "Well, I'm really glad you moved here from Chicago, Amy Iris Silverman. Not everyone wants to be friends with a weight-lifting girl with blue hair who knits animal hats."

Amy almost said she was glad she moved here from Chicago, but she stopped herself. "Yeah, only smart people would want to be friends with you."

Tate's cheeks turned pink. "Aw, thanks."

"I'm glad I walked into the library yesterday," Amy said. "Not everyone wants to be friends with . . ." She almost said *a girl with a leg-length discrepancy*. "A girl who lives in a funeral home and has hypergraphia."

Tate tilted her head. "You live in a funeral home and hyperwhoia?"

Amy worried she'd said too much. That was why she liked writing. She could always revise her written words and get them just right, but not so much with spoken words. "It's, um, my uncle's funeral home— Eternal Peace—and my dad and I moved in with him. And the word is 'hypergraphia.' You know, an obsessive need to write. That's me, Hypergraphia Girl." *Hypergraphia Girl?* Oh, how Amy wished there were a delete key on her mouth.

"Gotcha." Tate nodded. "I think it's cool that you love writing so much. I'll have to read your stories sometime. And who wouldn't want to be friends with you?"

Lots of people. Amy thought about the girls in the cafeteria who got up and walked away when she sat at their table the other day. And about how Kat was her only friend her age back in Chicago.

But here was Tate, this stylish, weight-lifting, super-fun girl with her own business knitting animal hats, who wanted to be her friend.

Amy understood Tate hadn't expected an answer to that last question.

And who wouldn't want to be friends with you?

She also knew that because of Tate Elizabeth Victoria McAllister, things were looking up in Buckington. Amy had made her first friend her own age.

And who wouldn't want to be friends with you?

Tate's words tap-danced through the happiness centers in Amy's brain, tripping joy switches left and right.

And who wouldn't want to be friends with you?

Those lovely words played on repeat in Amy's mind, propelling her one giant step closer to reaching her goal of a happy ending to her own story.

Another Chapter in Which Miles Spagoski Finds Something to Worry About

At the bowling center, Miles's mom pulled him behind the front counter and ducked down, as though she were on a secret spy mission. "You ready for Pop's seventy-fifth-birthday party next weekend?"

Miles nodded. He was ready, although he'd need next week to earn about twenty-five more dollars so he'd have exactly the amount needed to give his grandpop the best present ever.

"Good. Let's go over the plans." His mom looked toward the snack counter, then ducked a little lower. Even though they were far from where his grandfather was sitting, Miles's mom whispered. "Mercedes will arrive Thursday, the day before the party."

Miles couldn't help grinning. He'd missed his sister

since she left for college in August. And he'd never admit it to her, but he was so disappointed when she went skiing in Vermont with her roommate's family over winter break instead of coming home. Mercedes always managed to calm Miles's fears and tell him he was being a nincompoop when he worried too much.

"So here's the plan." His mom grabbed Miles's shoulders. "Stick promised to take Pop out for a long dinner at the Dining Car and keep him out so we can get everything ready here at the lanes. Your dad even bought a disco ball to hang for the party."

"Dad's weird," Miles said.

"I know. I thought you and Mercedes could act as lookouts for when they return so we can all leap out and yell 'Surprise!' Sound good?"

Miles bit his lower lip. "You think that'll be okay . . . for Pop's heart?"

Miles's mom stood tall and tousled his hair. "You, my dear son, worry entirely too much."

"But—"

"I know. I know. But Pop's been fine since his heart attack. I mean, a little crankier, but fine."

Miles shrugged. The doctors said his grandpop had lost about 50 percent of the functioning of his heart. That sounded like a lot of functioning to Miles. And a roomful of people yelling at a seventy-five-year-old man who'd had a heart attack seemed like a risky proposition to him. "Maybe we shouldn't do the yelling part when Pop walks in."

"Oh, Miles." His mom gently knocked her hip into his. "Loosen up. That's the best part of a surprise party."

Miles nodded, but he knew he'd worry about it before he fell asleep at night. He didn't understand why his mom wasn't more worried.

She let out a big breath. "Your grandpop will love having all his friends and family together."

Miles glanced at his grandfather, bent over a drink, on his special seat at the snack counter. "He will. It's just that—"

"Miles!" His mom put a hand on his shoulder. "Everything will be fine, and this surprise party should cheer him up."

"If it doesn't kill him."

"Miles!"

He hadn't meant to say that out loud. "Sorry."

"He'll be fine," she whispered sharply.

"I know." *But will he?* "I was only kidding."

"Come here."

Miles took a step closer to his mom.

Lane Spagoski enveloped him in a tight hug and swayed back and forth.

As she was smothering him with love, a bunch of his grandpop's buddies wheeled in.

His mom turned toward them. "Hey, everyone! You're all set up for lanes 47 and 48. Have a ball. Ha ha!"

Miles groaned at his mom's tired joke.

As the gang wheeled their chairs past, bowling bags in their laps, they waved. "Hey, Lane! Hi there, Miles!"

Miles waved.

He knew how happy this American Wheelchair Bowling Association league made his grandpop—he and Bubbie Louise had started it at Buckington Bowl a long time ago.

Miles didn't want to go home by himself tonight—he knew he'd just worry about the "Surprise!" part of his grandfather's party—so he kept busy straightening racks of bowling balls, pushing in chairs and helping his dad clean the grill until they said good night to Tyler, turned off all the video games and lights, helped his grandfather get situated in his wheelchair and left together.

But being in the house with his family didn't help.

Miles's panicked thoughts still took over when he tried to fall asleep. What if his mom was wrong? What if his grandfather did suffer a heart attack from the shock of all those people yelling at him? What if Miles never got a chance to give his grandpop the gift he'd been saving for? What if . . . ?

Miles wondered if there was one other person in all of Buckington who worried about things as much as he did. He got out of bed and scoured the Internet for weird ways people have died.

A man from New Zealand died when he slipped on some ice in his house and drowned in his cat's water bowl.

In 1854, a thirteen-year-old boy died when a circus clown swung him around by his heels.

In 1131, Crown Prince Philip of France died while riding through Paris, when his horse tripped over a black pig that was running out of a dung heap.

Somehow, the odd stories relaxed Miles enough that he was finally able to fall asleep.

FRAME 6   FRAME 7   FRAME 8   FRAME 9   FRAME 10

FRAME SIX

One of the Greatest Stories Ever Bowled

FRAME 6   FRAME 10

FRAME 6   FRAME 10

FRAME 6   FRAME 10

FRAME 6   FRAME 7   FRAME 8   FRAME 9   FRAME 10

FRAME 6   FRAME 7   FRAME 8   FRAME 9   FRAME 10

FRAME 6   FRAME 7   FRAME 8   FRAME 9   FRAME 10

Waffles and Weight Lifting

The minute Amy heard her dad's car pull into the driveway, she rushed down the steps of Eternal Peace Funeral Home, removed the velvet rope that hung across the stairs and charged toward the front door.

Wrapped in a thick parka, Amy's dad enveloped her in his bearlike arms and held her close.

Amy had forgotten her dad's brisk, clean smell. She'd forgotten the feel of his not-quite-soft beard on her face. She'd forgotten his tired, kind eyes, which looked especially tired tonight. She'd forgotten the tinge of sadness that had been in those eyes ever since her mom died.

Amy soaked it all in. "I'm so glad you're back, Dad. I missed you."

He squeezed Amy even tighter. "It's so good to be back, baby girl. I missed you something fierce."

She let his words fill her.

Uncle Matt shuffled over in his bathrobe and slippers. His presence interrupted their special moment, but Amy was so happy to have her dad back for the weekend she didn't mind. She stepped away so Uncle Matt could say hello, too.

"Hey there," he said, extending a hand to his brother.

Amy's dad grabbed Uncle Matt's hand and pulled him into a hug. The two men pounded each other on the back. When they broke apart, Uncle Matt asked, "So, how's the training going?"

Amy's dad whipped off his knit cap and ran his fingers through his curly brown hair. "It's an intense program, but I'm learning a lot. I'll be ready to get to work here with you in a couple more weeks."

"Terrific," Uncle Matt said. "I could sure use you around here. It's been hard since two part-time employees quit on me at the same time. Sheesh. The death care business isn't what it used to be."

"We've got this, bro." Amy's dad grabbed Uncle Matt into another hug.

"It's good to have you home." Uncle Matt held his brother at arm's length, looked into his eyes and nodded. "Well, I'm going up to bed. I'm pooped. See you two in the morning."

"Good night, Uncle Matt." Amy was glad to be left alone with her dad. Even though she could tell that he was impossibly tired, he agreed to watch a movie with her in the den.

Nestled in the warmth of her dad's arms, Amy didn't care about what was on the screen. She fell asleep twice and could barely drag herself up to the bed-that-smelled-like-mold when the movie ended. She sighed into her flat pillow, knowing tomorrow would be a special day with her dad.

She'd waited all week, and he was finally here.

As Amy drifted off to sleep, her happy feelings were mixed with sadness. She knew her dad would have to leave again in two days to go back to the mortuary school for his training. Only two days together, then five days apart.

She decided to make the most of their two days together.

• • •

Amy's dad slept so late Saturday morning, she had a chance to finish all her homework and play around with a poem she'd been working on. She wasn't going back to her story just yet. She was letting her subconscious work out what would happen next. When a good idea presented itself, she'd return to it.

In the meantime, Amy was happy to tinker with the poem. It was about her mom—how her superpower was making other people feel good about themselves.

When that poem felt finished, Amy wrote a new one, about learning to knit. It had an entirely different mood from the one about her mom. This one was lighter and had the rhythm of knitting needles clacking together.

LEARNING TO KNIT

Fingers fumble.
Clack. Clack. Clack.
Soft things connect.
Clack. Clack. Clack.
A stitch is missed.
Clack. Clack. Clack.
Redo. Rework.
Clack. Clack. Clack.
Rows of stitches.
Clack. Clack. Clack.
Perfect stitches.
Clack. Clack. Clack.
Pot holder born!

Amy loved how things from her life filtered into her writing in the most unexpected ways.

Finally, her dad poked his head into her bedroom. "I'm starving, Pumpkin. You ready for breakfast?"

Amy pointed at the time on her clock.

"Lunch, then? You ready for lunch?"

"I'm ready for blunch," Amy said.

"Blunch it is!"

"Dad?"

"Yes, ma'am?"

"My friend Tate is in a weight-lifting competition this afternoon. She asked if we'd like to go watch her."

"A friend?" One bushy eyebrow arched. "Weight-lifting competition?"

"Yes and yes," Amy said. "Do you want to go?"

"Do you?"

The truth was, Amy wanted to stay home and have her dad all to herself. But she also wanted to be a good friend and support Tate. "Yes!"

"Then it's a date. Do we have time for me to make us blunch?"

Amy nodded. "Definitely."

Blunch was blueberry waffles—lots of blueberry waffles—with sliced bananas and strawberries on top, all smothered in warm maple syrup. Just the smell of it made Amy happy.

Dad is home.

After blunch, they went to Tate's weight-lifting competition, and Amy's dad met Tate and her parents.

Amy loved seeing Tate lift weights right along with the male competitors. Tate's focus was intense. She looked different, Amy thought, when she wasn't wearing her penguin hat. When Tate won a medal for her age group, Amy cheered. She reminded herself to make sure her character Fiona, in the story she was writing, was as strong as Tate.

Amy's dad high-fived her. "Wow. She's amazing."

"Yes, she is." Amy pulled her shoulders back, feeling proud of her new friend. She remembered Tate's words: *And who wouldn't want to be friends with you?*

Beaming, Tate waved her medal at Amy.

Amy gave her a double thumbs-up, feeling happier than she'd thought possible.

After the competition ended, Tate handed her instant camera to her mom and had her take two photos of her with Amy, who was holding up the medal Tate had just won.

Each girl took a photo home as a souvenir.

The day was even more wonderful than Amy had hoped.

From Bumbershoot to Bowling

As great as Amy felt when her dad came home Friday evening, that was how awful she felt when he had to leave again Sunday. He needed several hours to drive back that night so he could get up early Monday morning to attend his first class.

The only thing that made school on Monday bearable for Amy was lunchtime in the library. Tate. Jelly Krimpets. Mr. Schu. Books.

It was hard on Amy to head back to Eternal Peace after school, knowing she wouldn't see her big bear of a dad again until Friday night, wouldn't be able to lose herself in his strong arms, would have to settle for a couple of texts and some quick, tired conversations at night.

It wasn't fair.

All the Jelly Krimpets in the world couldn't make up for how unfair it was.

When Amy was close enough to see the line of cars in the parking lot at Eternal Peace, she gasped. This was worse than unfair.

Since there was obviously a wake taking place, Amy slipped in through the back door, walked through the kitchen, avoided looking at the room where people were gathering and tiptoed upstairs. She understood she had to be quiet. Silent. Both her uncle and her dad had made that clear the first day. Nothing could ever disrupt a funeral.

Amy wouldn't want to do anything to disturb a funeral. A funeral was hard enough without someone making it worse.

So she pulled out her notebook and purple pen, climbed onto her bed-that-smelled-like-mold and got to work. She knew writing was the only thing that could distract her from what was happening one floor below.

Gratefully, Amy returned to the town of Bumbershoot, along with feisty Fiona and her three-legged dog, Lucky.

With all the big, smelly men grouped in front of the trembling duo near the drawbridge, the first man shouted, "She has Prince Harry's shoe!"

Fiona thought he'd said "Prince Hairy," and she almost giggled from the mistake and from her fear, but the man's next two words silenced her.

"Seize them!"

Before Fiona could think of fleeing, she and Lucky were scooped up roughly and carried, screaming and yelping, across the massive drawbridge and into the musty gray castle. The two were hauled up, up, up the dark, dank stone stairway that led to a foreboding door. One guard pushed the door open and another tossed Fiona and her dog into a tiny tower cell.

Before she and Lucky could determine the damage to themselves from such rough handling, a smelly brute snatched the shoe from Fiona's fingers, exited the room and shut the great door behind him, locking it with a loud clang.

Fiona cradled her whimpering dog in the crook of her arm and crawled to the narrow window. She looked out at the quarter moon, which cast barely a ray of hope into the inky night sky. And she thought of her poor father, alone and worried and probably hungry, like she and Lucky were now. She imagined her father had eaten boiled cabbage for dinner, like they did most nights. She'd love to have even a small bowl of that right now. Fiona also felt impossibly thirsty. And she knew Lucky felt that way, too, because he was panting and his tiny tongue was dangling from the side of his mouth.

Fiona settled onto the damp, cold floor with her furry friend curled in her lap. She absolutely, resolutely refused to cry. She wouldn't give her captors the satisfaction and she didn't want to waste even a drop of precious moisture on tears.

Then Fiona heard a deep, troubling wail from the floor below.

Wait a minute.

That last part didn't happen in the story.

So where had the disturbing wail come from?

From the floor below, Amy heard another deep, keening wail that seemed to shred her heart. It was the saddest sound in the universe.

She was familiar with that awful sound from her own experience at her mom's funeral. And Amy couldn't just sit there and listen to the howl of someone's deepest pain. She couldn't bear being reminded of her mom's funeral. Her tender heart, she knew, wouldn't survive it.

There it was again—that wounded wailing.

No. No. Nooooo!

Amy leapt off the bed. She donned her sneakers. She grabbed her coat and shrugged it on. Then she silently descended the richly carpeted stairs, willing

176

herself not to hear or see what was happening in the room at the bottom.

She zipped through the hallway, the kitchen, and the laundry room and out the back door.

Then, finally, she breathed. Deeply. The cold air woke her fully. She was in the parking lot, near the hearse that would soon hold the coffin that held the body.

She had to keep going.

Shivering, blinking, sniffing, Amy walked.

Before she knew it, she was standing in front of a Buckington icon. Not the Buckington Bed & Breakfast, because she'd remembered Tate would be visiting her aunt after school. No. She stood in front of Buckington Bowl, wondering how she'd even gotten there.

But if Amy were to be honest, she'd admit that the warmth and fun sounds of the bowling center attracted her as much as the coldness and horrible sounds of the funeral home repelled her. Plus—to be really, really honest—Amy was curious about Miles. She wanted to see him again.

Amy focused on a sign that said No Gum Allowed, then walked through the automatic doors, which parted for her, welcoming her like open arms.

The moment she stepped inside, the oldies music, the bright lights and the worn carpet with its color-ful shapes all felt familiar. She smiled at the woman she now knew was Miles's mom. She walked to the snack counter, deciding she'd order one hot chocolate in honor of her own mom, take her time drinking it, then head back. The woman at the funeral home would surely be done wailing by then. Maybe the whole funeral would be over. Amy hoped so.

"What can I get for you?" the man with the towel draped over his shoulder—Miles's dad—asked in a kind, cheerful way.

"Hot chocolate, please," Amy said.

He knocked twice on the countertop. "With marshmallows. You got it."

Amy smiled as he went back into the kitchen. It felt like her mom was there, somehow, making sure she was taken care of. While Amy waited for her hot chocolate with marshmallows, she nodded at Miles's grandfather. Then she walked over to the big board of photos, under the banner that read "The Greatest Stories Ever Bowled."

There were so many photos. So many people in those photos. Some smiling, some not. And right in the center was an older-looking photo of a woman sitting on the lap of a man in a wheelchair.

"That's my wife," Miles's grandfather said, holding up his mug, as if to say *Cheers!* to her memory.

"She's beautiful," Amy said, touching the edge of the black-and-white photo with her fingertip.

"Yes, she was." Miles's grandfather nodded. "Inside and out."

"I'll drink to that," said a man shooting pool from his wheelchair, even though the man didn't have a drink in his hand, only a pool cue.

"Me too," said Miles's grandfather, and he slurped from his mug.

"Drink to what?" someone asked.

Amy turned from the photos, from the stories she was eager to know more about, and saw Miles—his curly brown hair a little like her dad's, his thin lips, his slightly worried expression.

"Oh, um, hi," he said.

"Planning on spilling another soda on the poor girl?" Miles's grandfather asked, laughing.

Amy suppressed a giggle and returned to her stool at the counter.

Miles didn't laugh. "I just thought I'd stop over to say hi. Maybe I shouldn't have."

"Oh, come on," his grandfather said. "I was kidding. Don't be so sensitive."

Miles shrugged and sat next to Amy at the counter.

"Here's your hot chocolate." Miles's dad placed a steaming mug on the counter in front of Amy. "Plenty of marshmallows."

She pulled a few singles from her pocket and laid them on the counter. "Thanks."

179

Miles's dad scooped them up and wrapped on the counter with two knuckles again. He pointed at Miles. "Root beer for you, kiddo?"

Miles glanced at Amy. "Um, no thanks. I'm good."

"Smart choice, kid." Grandpop Billy chuckled and held up his mug. "Hey, how 'bout a refill for an old man?"

Miles's dad grabbed the towel off his shoulder and swiped at the counter. "How about I'll bring you a fresh cup of coffee if you agree to some improvements around here."

Grandpop Billy groused and grumbled.

"Ah, never mind, Pop." Miles's dad took the mug. "One cup of freshly brewed coffee coming right up."

"I'll take a burger and fries, George," the man called from his wheelchair near the pool table.

"You got it, Stick. Give me a few minutes to get the grill going."

"Appreciate it, my man."

Miles's dad knocked twice on the counter and disappeared into the kitchen.

The banter fascinated Amy. She always paid attention to conversations, thinking they might make good, realistic dialogue in future stories. Amy inhaled the sounds and smells and sights of the bowling center, then blew on her hot chocolate and watched steam spiral and swirl.

Her shoulders relaxed.

"You like to bowl?" Miles asked.

She almost said *I like to write,* but she didn't want him to think she was weird. Did she like to bowl? She remembered how much fun she had the few times her mom took her bowling, how her mom taught her to hold the ball properly and how they laughed between frames at their terrible scores. "Yes," Amy said. "I guess so."

Miles turned his back to his grandfather and spoke quietly to Amy. "When you're finished with your hot chocolate, you want to play a game?"

Amy felt her forehead tingle. A boy was asking her to bowl. Was this a date? Her first?

Answer the poor boy already, sweets.

Amy hadn't realized she was sitting there staring at Miles. Sometimes she forgot she wasn't the only one observing people; they could see her, too. "Oh, um, sure. But I have to warn you, I'm not any good." Amy imagined Miles was terrific at bowling, since he wore bowling shoes to school and his family owned a bowling center.

"Not any good, huh?" Miles tapped his chin. "In that case, want to bet five bucks on the game?"

"Miles Louis Spagoski!" Grandpop Billy barked.

Miles startled. "Kidding, Pop. I was only kidding. Sheesh."

181

Miles's cheeks turned pink, which made Amy like him all the more.

Amy was feeling so good from the atmosphere in the bowling center and from hearing her mom's words in her head that she boldly said, "Okay, I'll play a game with you. But first you have to tell me one story about a photo from that board."

Miles leaned back. "You want me to tell you one of the greatest stories ever bowled?"

"Yup." Amy thought she'd made a reasonable request.

"Okay," Miles said. "See that photo of the lady in the jeans and white top?"

Amy squinted. "Yup."

"She came here every night to bowl. Some nights, she was on a league and would come in and bowl a couple games before her league play started. Some nights, there was no league and she'd practice for several games. She told some people that during league play, she planned to bowl a nine hundred series— three perfect games in a row."

"Wow," Amy said. "Is that even possible?"

"It is," Grandpop Billy interrupted. "Becoming more common all the time."

Miles gave him the side-eye. "It does happen," Miles said. "But I'll tell you, I'd be happy to bowl *one* perfect game. You know?"

She didn't. The few times Amy had bowled, she'd counted it a success when her ball didn't roll into the gutter. "I guess." She took a good look at the photo. "Did she do it?"

"Well, that's the weird part," Miles continued. "One night for league play, she bowled a perfect game and people gathered around to watch. Then she bowled her second perfect game. It was unbelievable." His eyes grew wide. "She was on a total strike streak. Right, Pop?"

"He speaks the truth," his grandfather said. "It was a sight to behold."

Miles's dad put a fresh cup of coffee in front of his dad. "And your food's coming right up, Stick."

"Thanks, George."

When Miles's dad went back into the kitchen, Miles finished the story. "So we're all holding our breath for her third game. Everyone is absolutely quiet. And she gets strike after strike and people start whispering, 'She's going to do it.'"

Amy leaned closer. Her writer curiosity kicked in completely.

"Then, with three frames left to bowl, the woman takes her ball and puts it in her bag, changes into her street shoes and walks out."

"What?" Amy put her hands on her head. "She was that close to getting three perfect games in a row and she just walked away?"

"Yup." Miles scratched his head. "It was the weirdest thing. No one could figure it out."

"But that's no kind of ending, Miles. What happened the next time you saw her? Did she explain why she left like that? Did she get an important phone call? Was she sick?"

"No one knows," Miles's grandfather said.

Miles nodded. "She never came back."

"Is that true?" Amy asked.

"Absolutely true," Miles's grandfather said.

"Wow." Amy took a few swallows of her hot chocolate. "That was actually a great story, but I'm dying to find out what happened to her."

"I know. Me too," Miles said.

"Me too," Miles's grandfather said. "But some things will always remain a mystery. Isn't that right, Louise?"

Amy leaned closer to Miles. "Who's Louise?"

Miles's cheeks grew pink. "Hey, let's bowl. Meet me on lane forty-eight." He got off his stool and pointed toward the last lane. "I'll be right there."

Amy scooted off the stool, took a breath for bravery—because this totally felt like a first date—and walked to the farthest lane. She sat on a chair and checked her phone. No messages. She tried to imagine what might have made that woman leave when she was so close to bowling three perfect games in a row. Maybe Miles's grandfather was right. Some things in life would always be a mystery.

Miles arrived at lane 48 dragging his bowling bag and holding a pair of women's bowling shoes up to Amy.

She took them from him and saw the number $8\frac{1}{2}$ on the backs. "Um, how'd you know my size?"

Miles smiled. "It's sort of my superpower. I'm really good at guessing people's shoe sizes."

"That's an unusual superpower."

Miles changed from his street bowling shoes into the ones for the lanes.

Feeling self-conscious, Amy quickly yanked off her sneaker with the heel lift and shoved it under the chair. She slipped into the bowling shoes, which fit perfectly but felt heavy and clunky.

Miles told Amy to go first, so she did, but was uncomfortable. It seemed so obvious to Amy that her right leg was shorter than her left. She wished she hadn't agreed to bowl with Miles. They should have stayed at the snack counter, and he could have told her more stories about the people in the photographs on the bulletin board.

Amy was so focused on herself and not on what she was doing that she managed to bowl a total of six gutter balls on her first three turns.

Miles, on the other hand, bowled three strikes in a row. He gave a fist pump and shouted, "Turkey!"

"Yes, you are," Grandpop Billy called from his seat at the counter.

Amy didn't think Miles was a turkey. "Hey," Amy said. "I think you have another superpower. You're really good at bowling."

Miles stumbled, then steadied himself. "Um, thanks. But I'm not that good. Not yet, anyway. I'm still working toward my first perfect game."

"You're not hustling that nice girl, are you?" Grandpop Billy yelled.

Miles sank low in the chair next to Amy and covered his face with his hands.

"Your grandfather's funny," Amy said.

"Yeah." Miles glanced back, then shook his head. "Hilarious."

"Should I, um, take my turn?" Amy asked.

"Please," Miles said.

And they continued to play.

At the end of their second game, Amy kept rubbing her left hip.

She noticed Miles peeking under the chair at her sneaker, the one with the heel lift. His gaze lingered too long. She felt something inside herself crumble, like he'd managed to peer inside her and view the most sensitive part.

When Miles turned back and saw the look on Amy's face, he blurted, "Did you know that in 1974 a guy named Basil Brown died from drinking too much carrot juice?"

"What? Huh?" Amy shook her head, trying to convince herself it didn't matter that Miles was looking at her sneaker. That it wouldn't make him think differently about her. That it was such a small part of who she was.

"It's true," Miles said. "He died from drinking too much carrot juice."

Amy sat on the chair next to Miles, glad to take the weight off her aching hip. "How can that be?" she asked. "Aren't carrots supposed to be good for you?"

"Yes," Miles said, "but he drank a gallon of carrot juice every day for ten days, plus he took vitamin A supplements. Way too many. Really dangerous. It ruined his liver."

"That's fascinating," Amy said.

Miles let out a breath. "It is?"

"Well, I think it is. Unusual stories like that always interest me."

Miles sat a little taller. "I guess it *is* a cool story." Miles offered one more odd fact. "Basil was bright yellow when he died."

"No way."

"Yep. Big Bird yellow."

Amy cracked up at the image. She considered telling Miles she lived over a funeral home because she thought he might appreciate the odd fact, but then she worried he'd think it was weird. "Well, I'd better go," Amy said, even though she didn't want to leave.

"Um, okay. Want me to walk you?"

"You want to walk me? Home?" Amy reminded herself that Eternal Peace was not her home, but a place she had to live for now. And she wasn't ready for Miles to see where she was living.

"Sure," Miles said. "It's dark out."

"I'm not afraid of the dark," Amy said.

"No, I know. I just thought—"

"I'll be okay," Amy said. "Thanks, though. And thanks for the bowling. It was fun. Sorry I was so bad at it."

"You were great," Miles said.

"Um, right." Amy put on her sneakers quickly, handed Miles the bowling shoes and shrugged on her coat. "Well, see you around, Miles Louis Spagoski."

"Bye, Amy."

As Amy walked toward the doors, Miles yelled, "Don't drink too much carrot juice!"

Amy laughed and gave a little wave. She heard Miles's grandfather yell, "Smooth line there, Casanova!"

Outside, as cold air hit her face, Amy inhaled

deeply and realized she felt so much better than when she'd walked in. "Carrot juice." She shook her head and smiled. Then she walked back toward the funeral home, whistling, and rubbing her aching hip every so often.

The cold air felt delicious on her warm cheeks.

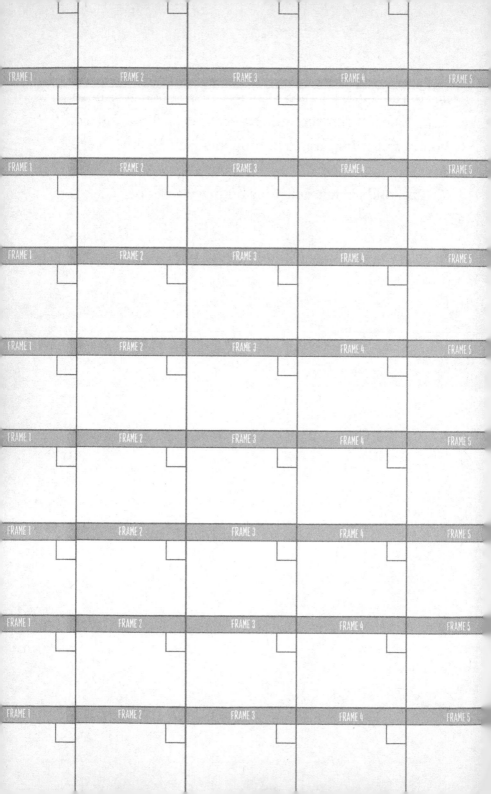

FRAME SEVEN

Surprise!

Miles's New Obsession

That night in bed, Miles didn't obsess about death and dying.

Instead, he obsessed about something else. Or, to be more accurate, some*one* else: Amy.

Miles worried his last comment about the carrot juice was so idiotic it ruined all the good times that had come before it. He wished he'd said something smart and smooth, but the carrot-juice line was what spilled from his mouth. He hoped Amy didn't hold it against him.

Mostly, though, Miles kept thinking about the heel lift on Amy's sneaker. He thought about how she had an uneven approach when she wore bowling shoes. Miles remembered how she had rubbed her hip at the end of the second game, like it hurt, but she never complained or even mentioned it. And she'd seemed to be having a good time with him. At least, he hoped so.

Then he remembered something wonderful. Before he'd joined Amy at the snack counter, Miles had bowled with a few guys and won the rest of the money he needed to get the special gift for his grandpop's seventy-fifth-birthday party.

He let out a long, slow breath. He was done hustling people on the lanes for good. That was one less thing he'd have to be nervous about.

Maybe he'd set up a business helping people work on their technique and bring up their averages. He wasn't sure whether people would pay him, because he was a kid, but he knew he could help them improve. And his parents had told him he could start hosting the little-kid birthday parties on weekends. He'd have to set up tables in the party room, serve pizza and pitchers of soda, make sure the kids got their rental shoes and clean up when the party was over. After those parties, the parents almost always tipped the host.

Things were working out. Miles had gotten the money for his grandpop's gift in time, he was done hustling and he'd had a nice time with Amy. Except for his stupid carrot-juice line and Amy rubbing her hip, it was perfect.

Maybe the bowling shoes he wore to school every day *were* lucky.

A Story in Which Things Get, Um, Hairy

When Amy got back to Eternal Peace, the parking lot was nearly empty. She let out a big breath.

In the kitchen, her uncle was poring over papers at the table.

"Hey, Uncle Matt."

He startled. "Oh, hi, Ames!" His voice was bright, but his eyes looked tired. "Thanks for texting so I knew where you were. Did you have a good time bowling?"

Amy slid onto a seat at the table and thought about how much she'd enjoyed bowling with Miles and hearing his stories. "I had a really good time."

"Glad to hear that." Uncle Matt patted her hand. "I hope you grow to like it here in Buckington."

Amy offered a weak smile. *I really hope we don't*

stay long enough for me to like it here. My life is back in Chicago.

"Want an egg salad sandwich?" he asked.

Amy suddenly realized she was starving. "Please."

The two of them ate egg salad sandwiches on sourdough bread, with a sliced kosher pickle on the side and chocolate pudding pie for dessert.

Then Amy let her uncle get back to his paperwork and went up to her room. After texting with her dad and Kat, she pulled out her notebook and purple pen. Her unfinished story had been tickling her mind all day, feeling like an itch desperately needing to be scratched.

So she scratched it by writing.

Fiona was at the point of panic, worrying about how she'd get out of the cell high up in the castle's tower. She was hungry, thirsty, sore and exhausted, and she knew her dog must be all those things, too. While grateful for Lucky, Fiona felt bad for taking him along on her foolish adventure. She should have left him back home with her father, where he could be safe and cozy in their cabin. Fiona realized she should have gone alone or maybe stayed home, too. Then she and Lucky wouldn't be trapped.

The heavy door to their cell creaked open.

Fiona's grip on Lucky tightened, and she backed up so her spine pressed against the damp stone wall.

Then the most unusual creature entered.

The creature was no larger than a boy her age. But it wasn't like any boy Fiona had ever seen.

"Hello," the creature said. "I'm Prince Harry."

Again Fiona thought she heard the words "Prince Hairy," and this time it would have made perfect sense.

The creature standing before her was covered with long brown hair. His face. His arms. The backs of his hands. All covered with hair. He looked more wolf than boy. "Prince . . . Prince . . . Har—"

"You think I'm hideous!" the prince cried. "I knew you would. Everyone does." He covered his hairy face with his palms and let out a deep wail.

Fiona placed Lucky on the floor and stepped forward. "I do not," she said, although she was still trying to figure out what she thought.

"Then you would be the only one." Prince Harry sniffed and wiped his hairy nose on his hairy forearm, leaving a sheen of snot, which Fiona found a tiny bit repulsive. "No one wants to be around me," Prince Harry moaned. "Not the kids my age, not the servants or the guards who work here. Not even my own father."

Fiona wondered what the prince's mother thought of him. She noticed he hadn't mentioned her.

"Oh, that can't be true," Fiona said. "Parents love you no matter what."

"Not always," the prince muttered.

And somehow, Fiona knew this to be true.

The prince looked up at Fiona, and she saw that, behind all the hair, he had the most compelling green eyes. Eyes that were both a deep mystery and a shining light all at once.

Feeling brave, Fiona thrust out her hand. "I'm Fiona, the one who found your shoe."

The prince took Fiona's hand gently and kissed the back of it. The hair on his face tickled her hand. "You know," he said, "I lost the shoe doing something I shouldn't have."

Fiona was beginning to like Prince Harry.

"I thought princes always did what they were supposed to. May I ask what you did that you shouldn't have?"

The prince let out a little laugh. "Oh, I simply wanted to be normal."

Fiona nodded, to encourage him to go on.

Lucky went over and sniffed the tops of the prince's feet.

The prince bent down and petted Lucky, who rolled onto his back to be scratched on his belly—something he rarely did unless he trusted someone completely. Lucky was a good judge of character. Fiona thought this was a positive sign.

"Here's what happened," the prince said. "Even though

my father—you know, the king—said I must never leave the castle grounds, I disobeyed him."

Fiona leaned forward. She had a feeling this would be a good story.

The prince continued: "Not only did I leave the castle grounds, as I was strictly forbidden to do, but I walked and walked and then walked some more. Freedom felt wonderful! I passed towns and fields and farm animals who didn't care I was covered with more hair than they were."

Fiona couldn't help giggling at this image. She covered her mouth with her hand, so as not to appear rude.

"It's okay," Prince Harry said. "You can laugh. I meant it to be funny."

Fiona lowered her hand.

"Anyway, it was one of the best days of my life," Prince Harry said. "Until . . ." The prince stared off into whatever lay beyond the tower window.

"Until what?" Fiona needed to know.

Lucky barked. Maybe Lucky wanted to know, too.

The prince shook his head. "Until I came upon a bunch of boys. They thought it was hilarious that I was half human, half beast."

"Oh, you're not any part beast," Fiona said. She hadn't meant to interrupt the prince's story.

The prince smiled. "I wish you could have told that to those boys. They tackled me and . . ." Harry looked down, unable to go on.

Fiona gasped. "But . . . but . . . you're a prince!"

"They didn't know nor care who I was."

"Idiots!"

"Indeed. And one of them yanked off my shoe and threw it as hard as he could. It flew in a great arc." Prince Harry let out a long breath. "Once they finally left me alone, I searched for it, but I couldn't find my missing shoe. I knew it would get dark in a couple hours. So, half shoeless, I hobbled all the way back to the castle. In fact, I arrived here only an hour before you showed up. Just long enough for the king to . . ." Prince Harry didn't finish his sentence.

"Oh, I'm so sorry," Fiona said. "That must've felt terrible. People can be so cruel." She ran up to the prince and hugged him tightly. His hair was soft and smelled nice.

"Not . . . everyone . . . is . . ." The prince hiccupped and swiped at his eyes. "Cruel."

Fiona wiped his tears away with the edge of her apron, making sure not to use the part with dried blood on it.

"Your kindness . . ." The prince sniffed. "Kindness isn't something I experience often. How do I return the favor?"

The question startled Fiona. She couldn't believe someone as exalted as a prince wanted to do something for her. She thought of the reward she'd hope to earn from returning the shoe with the shiny buckle, then looked at her surroundings and knew she needed something more basic. "Would you set me free?" Fiona looked at Lucky and had to hold in her own sniffles. "I have to get home to my father. He's all by himself."

The prince made a small gasp. "Have you no mother?"

Fiona shook her head.

"Nor do I," the prince said softly. "She passed a couple years ago. And she was like me." He motioned to the hair all over his face and body. "But she had her attendants remove the hair daily. I think it hurt her, but my father insisted. He felt she was beautiful only when her facial and body hair were gone. My mother told me many times to be proud of exactly who I am, but that's hard when . . . when . . . Well, I miss her every day."

"Oh," Fiona said, "I understand." And she did. "You can see why Lucky and I must get home to my father."

"I do," the prince said. "And I'm sorry, but that's one thing I can't make happen. That's up to the palace guards, and I know they'll let you go only when they're good and ready."

"But you're the prince," Fiona said. "Can you do nothing to get us out of here?"

Prince Harry shook his head. "After my escapade of running away, my father said he'd boil me alive if I broke another rule. I think he meant it, Fiona. He was . . . he was . . . Is there anything else I can do for you? Anything at all?"

Fiona turned her back to the prince for a moment to hide her disappointment. She was so worried about her father . . . but then a thought flickered. An idea. A possibility. It filled her with hope and a renewed sense of determination. Fiona whirled around. "Yes, there is something you can do for me."

"Oh, I'm pleased," the prince said, moving closer. "What is it?"

"You can get my dog and me a hearty meal and some drink. It's been a long journey. We're both famished."

"I can do that," the prince said. "They're usually good to me in the kitchen, as long as I don't get my hairy self too close to the food they're preparing."

"That's wonderful. Thank you. I'd like to do something for you," Fiona said, thinking of her idea.

"But . . . but . . . ," the prince sputtered. "Your kindness is enough." He looked down. "I couldn't let you do anything else for me. I don't deserve any more than that."

Fiona boldly tipped the prince's hairy chin up so he had to look at her with his brilliant green eyes. "Yes, I must do this one thing for you. And you must allow me to do it. It could change everything." Then Fiona thought: *It could change everything for both of us.*

"Well, what is it? What is this thing you want to do for me that might change everything?" He looked at Fiona with a burning intensity.

Fiona recognized that look, that desperate need for things to change, for things to get better. She took the prince's hairy hand into her own. "I'll tell you everything, Prince Harry, after you bring us something to eat and drink. We're practically starving and so, so thirsty. Right, Lucky?"

The little dog looked up and whimpered.

"Well then, let me attend to those things."

And with those words, the prince left Fiona and Lucky alone in their tower prison.

Amy felt exhausted when she unclenched her right hand and placed her pen and notebook on the desk. She loved the way this story was unfolding and couldn't wait to return to it and discover what Fiona's bright idea was. Amy knew that by the time she sat down to write again, her subconscious would have done the heavy lifting and figured it out.

When she checked her phone, she couldn't believe how late it was, how she'd lost track of time while writing. That happened sometimes.

Feeling quite satisfied with her writing self, Amy let out a long, slow breath. She thought again about what a fun time she'd had at the bowling center with Miles earlier.

Then, for the first time in a while, Amy let herself relax completely and slip into a deep and peaceful sleep.

Time is a brisk wind, for each hour it brings something new . . . but who can understand and measure its sharp breath, its mystery and its design? —PARACELSUS

We each have 86,400 seconds in a day, give or take an attosecond.*

But what does that mean? What does time really mean?

Isaac Newton and Albert Einstein offered theories to explain time. I'm sure you've studied them and come to your own confusions, er, conclusions.

Then tell me this, smarty pants: How does one explain the feeling that time moves at a glacial pace when one is sad and suffering? Or how time seems to pass in a blink when one is fully absorbed in an activity? Why does time seem to move too slowly when one is young and too quickly when one is old? And not at all when one is waiting for the school day to end on the Friday afternoon of a holiday weekend?

Time represents change. The planet keeps spinning, our bodies keep aging. Things keep changing, whether we notice or not.

That is the nature of time and also the mystery of it.

All this is to say, dear reader, time has passed in the story. Things have changed . . . even if the characters don't quite realize it yet.

---

* Attosecond = one quintillionth of a second. An attosecond is to a second what a second is to about 32 billion years. Isn't science fun?

A Short Time in Which Things Are All Right

Amy couldn't believe she'd made it to Friday night. She couldn't stand spending every day and night with her dad so far away.

When he walked in, smelling of the cold and of stale coffee, she lost herself in his bulky arms, his tight embrace.

"You know," her dad said, "we have only one more week of this baloney. Then I'll be done with training. I mean, as long as I pass the exam next Friday."

Amy looked into her father's tired eyes. "Oh, you'll pass."

"Is that so, Miss Ames?"

"No doubt." Amy hugged him again. "You have to pass, or all this work will have been for nothing. Right?"

Her dad tugged at his earlobe. "Right. Hey, did I tell you we spent one whole day this past week learning death care vocabulary?"

"What's that?"

"Different terminology used in the industry. Like calling a burial an 'interment' or a coffin a 'casket.' Sounds nicer, I suppose. And we spent an entire day on it, then had a test."

"How'd you do on the test?"

"Hundred percent."

"See, I told you you've got this. The final test will be a breeze for you. Now, on to the important question: Do you want popcorn or Popsicles for movie night?"

"Popcorn," her dad said. "It's too cold for Popsicles. Let me take off my coat, say hi to Uncle Matt and put my stuff away first."

"I'll get the popcorn started." Amy skipped through the hall of Eternal Peace Funeral Home to the kitchen, where she grabbed the biggest pot she could find and placed it on a burner. She rummaged through the pantry until she found the bag of popcorn they'd bought especially for Friday movie nights.

As she was heating oil in the pot, she looked up, as though she could see through the ceiling to the floor where her dad was putting his stuff away.

She took a moment to appreciate that her dad was home. Finally.

They were going to cuddle on the couch and watch a movie together.

She'd begun making friends.

She was writing a cool fairy tale.

She even had a new, fuzzy purple blanket, a soft sheet set and a fluffy pillow that felt like clouds and smelled like lavender, all because Uncle Matt took her shopping at Target the other day for "some things to make you feel more at home in your bedroom."

Everything, Amy knew, was as right as it could be.

Until, Dear Reader, it wasn't.

Because you don't need to be Isaac Newton or Albert Einstein to understand that time has a way of changing things. Even good things. And that the changes can happen during any one of those 86,400 seconds in a day, whether you are ready for them or not. We tend to think the way things are right now is the way they will be in the future, but that is faulty reasoning.

You are changing.

The world around you is changing.

And our story world, Dear Reader, is changing, too.

Even the ghosts of Isaac Newton and Albert Einstein could have told you that.

Party Time!

Friday evening, things were happening at Buckington Bowl.

Stick had taken Grandpop Billy to the Dining Car, down the street, as planned. After dinner and several cups of coffee, Stick rolled his wheelchair to the restroom to call Miles's mom and let her know the check had arrived and he wouldn't be able to keep the birthday boy there much longer.

"Okay," she said to the people assembled at the snack bar and in the billiard area. "I'll turn off the lights. We can all duck down, and when Billy rolls up, we'll jump and shout 'Surprise!'"

Miles gripped his sister's fingers entirely too tightly.

"Ow!" Mercedes shook her hand loose.

"Sorry," Miles muttered. He was still worried that shouting "Surprise!" at his seventy-five-year-old grandfather was a lousy idea. He thought about telling this to his mom for the hundredth time, but instead inhaled deeply and admonished himself to knock it off. Miles was trying to get a grip on his anxieties. His grandfather would be fine, he told himself. The surprise would make him happy. Miles's gift would make him even happier.

Then why did Miles feel anxious?

Randall nudged Miles's shoulder. "Hey, man, you really should ask the new girl to the dance."

"Amy?"

"Yeah." Randall straightened the lapel on his suit jacket, then gave his thin black tie a quick adjustment. "The girl we nearly knocked out with your bowling shoe."

"You mean the girl *you* nearly knocked out."

Randall shrugged. "Yeah, whatever. Tate tells me she really likes dancing."

"Amy?"

"Yes, Amy. Likes dancing." Randall raised an eyebrow. "Are you all there?" He knocked on Miles's forehead, and Miles jerked away.

"Stop!" He was still panicked about his grandfather. Plus, he thought of the heel lift in Amy's sneaker and wondered how dancing worked for her if she wore shoes without a lift. Was she off-balance, like when she bowled?

"You told me you two had a good time when you bowled together, and I think you should ask her to the dance. That way the four of us could go together."

"Right," Miles said. "But I don't like dancing. So there's that."

Tate, who was crouched in front of Randall, swiveled. "But that's irrelevant, Miles. You should totally ask her anyway. She's really nice. I hang out with her every day at lunch."

"But what if she says no?" Miles whispered, then was instantly sorry he'd let his one true thought slip out.

"Be brave, Miles," Tate said, and turned and winked at Randall. "Sometimes it pays off. Besides, Miles Spagoski, how could anyone resist you?" She reached up and pinched his cheek.

This annoyed Miles. He was too nervous for cheek pinching.

Randall shoved Miles. "Yeah. Be brave, man."

"Quiet!" Mercedes warned. "Pop will be here any second."

Miles was sure something terrible would happen to his grandfather, and his brain couldn't convince his sick stomach otherwise.

Tate leaned back and whispered: "I'm having a party at my house the night before the dance. You definitely have to come to that, Miles. It'll just be the four of us."

"Four?" For as long as Miles could remember, it had been the three of them hanging out together.

"Yeah," Tate said, as though it was no big deal. "You, me, Randall and Amy."

"Oh," Miles said. He liked Amy but wasn't sure how to feel about this new development. Letting someone else into their group was a big change, and no one had asked him how he felt about it. His stomach clenched.

"I'll be there," Randall said. "For sure."

"You'd better be." Tate punched him in the arm.

Randall rubbed the place where she'd punched him. "You realize your fists are lethal weapons, right?"

Tate grinned. "So I've been told."

Miles felt off-balance. Tate never had parties at her house. When the three of them got together, they always went to Randall's house or to the lanes to bowl and play video games. Miles imagined hanging out with Amy at Tate's house. The thought made him nervous and excited at the same time. "I guess it could be fun," he said.

"Shhhhh!" Miles's mom scolded.

"Sorry," Miles whispered. And he switched back to worrying about everyone poised to yell "Surprise!" at his grandfather.

Miles's mom patted his shoulder. "Everything will be fine."

His dad scooted out from the kitchen, whipped off his apron, laid it on the counter and crouched nearby. "Hey there, gang!"

"Shhh," Miles's mom said, but she was smiling and squeezing his dad's fingers, which rested lightly on her shoulder.

There was so much happy, nervous energy at the bowling center that when someone's cell rang, everyone screamed.

Then laughed.

"Shhh. Shhhhh!" warned Miles's cousin Jeanne, who'd been keeping watch at the door. "They're coming!" she called. "Rolling up right now!" Jeanne ran to the group of family and friends and crouched low.

It was so quiet at the bowling center that Miles could hear a soft, rattling wheeze coming from Randall. He wished Randall would take a puff from his inhaler, but he didn't dare say another word for fear his mom would scream at him and ruin the surprise for his grandfather—although Miles thought ruining the surprise might be a good idea. He knew getting a heart attack and dying at your own surprise party wouldn't be the strangest way someone had died. Recently, he had read about Aeschylus, often called the

Father of Tragedy because of the plays he wrote. But Miles thought the description was apt because of how the Greek playwright had died. Aeschylus perished in 456 BC when an eagle dropped a tortoise on his head. *A tortoise!* He'd been staying outdoors because of a prophecy that he'd be killed by a falling object.

The eagle apparently mistook Aeschylus's head for a rock that would shatter the tortoise's shell.

The tortoise reportedly survived.

Miles thought that if he did go to Tate's party—which he probably wouldn't—he might share the unusual story of Aeschylus with Amy. He had a feeling she'd appreciate it.

After hearing the automatic doors sliding open and wind whooshing in, Miles heard his grandfather grumble, "What's goin' on here? Why's the place dark on a Saturday night? Did the power go out or something?"

Miles's heart beat too fast. Maybe he shouldn't be worrying about his grandfather's heart, but about his own. *Please be okay, Pop. Please be okay, Pop. Please—*

Then he heard Stick's voice. "Well, I can't imagine what the—"

"SURPRISE!" everyone yelled.

Miles's heart jackhammered.

Someone flipped on the lights.

Miles's dad turned on the oldies rock music, which crackled through the speakers.

Cousin Jeanne threw handfuls of multicolored confetti into the air over Pop's wheelchair.

Miles watched his grandpop's face through the floating bits of confetti. It didn't look like he was stressed or panicked. He looked . . . happy, sad and overwhelmed all at once.

"Happy birthday, Pop," Miles's dad said, enveloping his father in a tight embrace.

Then Miles's mom kissed Pop on the cheek. "Happy birthday, old man. We love you."

When Mercedes stepped in front of their grandfather's wheelchair, Miles watched a tear slide down Pop's cheek. "Sweetheart!" Grandpop Billy said, opening his arms wide. "You came home from college."

"Of course!" she said. "I wouldn't miss your birthday, Pop."

"Well," he said, swiping at another tear. "I . . . Well."

"Oh, Pop!" Mercedes said, leaning down and hugging him.

"Don't begrudge an old man a good cry over his favorite granddaughter."

"But I'm your only—"

"Yeah," Grandpop Billy said. "Don't ruin the moment, Ms. Sassy Pants."

Then it was Miles's turn. When he fell into his grandfather's arms, Pop pounded him on the back. "You know I love you, kid."

Miles did know. It meant everything. He ached with wishing his bubbie Louise were still here. She would have been on Miles's grandfather's lap, he imagined, and they would have been spinning to whatever music was playing and laughing their joy out to the whole world.

When everyone at the party had had a chance to say "Happy birthday" and give him a hug or a kiss or squeeze his shoulder, Miles's grandfather looked out over the crowd and shook his head. "Wouldn't Louise have loved every minute of this?"

A chorus of *Awww*s went through the crowd.

After a big sniff, Billy croaked, "So let's get this party started. It's not every day you turn seventy-five. Somebody get me a drink!"

"Comin' right up, Pop," Miles's dad called.

And with that, the party at Buckington Bowl moved into full swing.

FRAME EIGHT

The Story
Behind the Story of Life,
Death and Bowling

The Part Where a Story Is Revealed, a Gift Is Given, and a Heart Is Broken

Miles's stomach tightened when his mom announced it was time for presents. This was it. He'd been working toward this moment for such a long time.

He decided to let everyone else give their gifts before him.

Stick went first. He rolled his wheelchair over and gave Grandpop Billy a box with a wide ribbon tied around it. Inside the box was a T-shirt that read "Beware an Old Fart with a Bowling Ball."

When Grandpop Billy held the shirt up, everyone laughed.

"Made that one just for you, my friend."

"You're quite a talent with a sewing machine, Stick."

"You got that right," Stick said. Then his face looked

more serious. "I'm sure glad the AWBA brought us to-gether, ya old fart."

"Me too," Grandpop Billy said, ducking his head. Then he pointed over at the center of the bulletin board. "But it really began with that lady. She's the one who convinced me to start an AWBA league here. Louise was the beginning of every good thing."

"To Louise!" Stick shouted.

People raised their glasses. "To Louise!"

"To Louise," Grandpop Billy whispered.

"Hey," Tate said. "This one's from me, Mr. Spa-goski."

"Well, thanks, sweetheart. When are you going to change your hair back to a normal color?"

Tate shrugged. "Thought the blue matched my penguin hat nicely."

Miles's grandfather laughed. "Indeed it does, sweet-heart. You know, you're the coolest friend Miles has." He nodded toward Randall. "No offense."

Randall tugged on his lapels, put one shiny sneaker behind the other, did a fancy spin and nodded at Grandpop Billy.

Grandpop Billy cracked up. "And *you're* his most stylish friend." He glanced at Tate. "No offense, sweet-heart."

"None taken," Tate said. "Now open my present."

Inside the box was the world's longest scarf.

Billy wrapped it around and around and around his neck. "I love it."

Tate blushed.

"But this could be a scarf for a giraffe. You know that, right?"

Tate smiled. "Guess I got carried away."

Mercedes gave her grandfather a framed photo of Bubbie Louise with her and Miles from several years ago, which made him pull out a handkerchief, swipe at his eyes and blow his nose. "It's beautiful, Mercedes. Don't mind me. I'm just a sentimental old fool."

Mercedes hugged her grandfather. "Love you, Pop."

"Love you, darlin'."

Miles's mom and dad gave Grandpop Billy an Eagles sweatshirt, since that was his favorite team (Go, Birds!), and a gift certificate to the Dining Car.

Randall presented him with a trophy. The plaque on it read "World's Crankiest Bowler," which made the whole crowd howl with laughter.

"So true," Grandpop Billy admitted, raising the trophy high. "So true."

After everyone else had given Grandpop Billy their gifts, Miles was about to approach when his grandfather held up his arms. "I think it's time to tell the story of how this all came to be."

"Let's hear the story!" someone shouted.

Miles would have to wait to give his grandfather the gift, but that was okay. He loved hearing this story.

Billy grabbed a pool cue, rolled his chair over and pointed to the photo at the center of the "Greatest Stories Ever Bowled" board. "So, one night, my sorry legless butt was sitting right there at the snack counter." He pointed to his usual seat. "The place was owned by Rock Trumbo and his wife, Kitty, back then."

A few of the old-timers nodded.

"Anyway, this gorgeous woman walks in with a couple of her girlfriends. She sits at the counter and orders a hot chocolate."

Miles let out a breath, thinking about Amy ordering a hot chocolate the other day.

Billy went on, "I was sitting on the other side from her and her friends, and my jaw near dropped down onto the counter."

Mercedes poked Miles's shoulder. "This story gets better every time."

Miles nodded, but wished he'd given his grandfather the gift before the story started so he wouldn't be thinking about it now.

"So naturally," Grandpop Billy said, "I started talking her up. Couldn't help myself. You all know I've got a big mouth."

"Indeed you do!" Stick shouted.

Everyone laughed.

"Okay, settle down. By the time she'd finished her hot chocolate and her friends were ready to go, I had her phone number. In this very hand," he said, waving his right hand, "was the number of an angel." Grandpop Billy let out a slow breath. "But the more I thought about it, the worse I felt, like I'd tricked her or something."

"Aw, this part always makes me sad," Mercedes whispered to Miles.

"Me too."

"We love you, Pop!" Miles's dad called out.

"Love you, too." Grandpop Billy pointed at his son with the pool cue. "So I called her, all right, but I told her the truth. I told her that she couldn't tell from where she was sitting at the counter, but I had lost both my legs from when that bus hit me." He hung his head for a few moments, as though he was remembering the accident that took his legs all those years ago. Then his head popped up. "And you know what she said? What that angel said to me?"

"What?" a few people called, even though everyone knew exactly what Louise had said because they'd all heard the story before.

Grandpop Billy swallowed. "She said, 'Why would

that make any difference? Why on earth would that make me not want to go out with you?'"

More *Awww*s from the crowd.

"Before I knew it, we were getting married. And because Louise loved this bowling center so much, when I got the settlement money from the bus company, I bought this old place from Rock and Kitty for my . . . my . . . Louise." Grandpop Billy sniffed.

"It's okay, Pop." Lane wrapped an arm around his shoulders.

Mercedes ran up and kissed him on the forehead.

Grandpop Billy squeezed their hands.

That was when Miles approached his grandfather and handed him the envelope, which was getting sweaty from being in his hands so long. "I have something for you, Pop. It's my gift for your birthday."

His grandfather smiled.

Miles couldn't believe how long he'd planned and worked for this moment. "Open it."

Billy weighed the envelope in his palm. "Hmm. It's got some heft to it, that's for sure, but it's too light to be a new car."

"Very funny," Miles said. He couldn't stand the suspense any longer. "Go ahead, Pop."

"Okay. Okay."

Miles bit his bottom lip while his grandfather slid a gnarled index finger under the flap.

Some people had gone to the snack bar. A few were bowling. Others were shooting a game of pool. But a bunch were still standing there, watching.

Grandpop Billy pulled out the paper that was inside. His lips moved as he read quietly. "All expenses . . . International Bowling Museum and Hall of Fame." Then he peered inside the envelope, which was stuffed with hundred-dollar bills. "I can't take this," Billy said, and handed it back to Miles. "Thank you."

Dumbfounded, Miles accepted the envelope and sputtered, "Don't—don't worry about the money, Pop. I saved it up all through the years. It's okay."

"It's not okay!" Grandpop Billy snapped. "That's not it. I can't take this. I don't want it." He waved the paper at Miles until he took it from his fingers. "I can't go there without her, Miles."

Now his grandfather started to cry. Really cry. Shoulders heaving.

People were paying attention.

"You won't have to go alone, Pop." A heaviness, like a bag of rocks, took up residence in Miles's stomach. "There's enough money in there for you to go with another person. I thought . . . well, maybe . . . I could go with you."

Billy Spagoski swiped an arm across his leaky eyes and barked, "I said NO!" And he wheeled himself away.

Miles, gripping the envelope, turned and saw the concerned looks on people's faces. He ran past them all and into the bathroom across from lane 48.

He considered flushing all the hundred-dollar bills down the toilet. Instead, he kicked the trash can. It fell over with a loud clang. But that wasn't satisfying enough, so he kicked a stall door so hard it hit the wall and came back at him. Before Miles could make mincemeat of the hand dryer or soap dispenser, Randall came huffing in. "What's going on?"

Miles crossed his arms over his chest. "I don't know why he's such a jerk! I worked forever for that!"

"Your grandpop?"

"Yes, my grandpop! I saved for that gift for years!" Miles kicked the trash can again for good measure. The only thing that accomplished was hurting his toes, but Miles didn't care about *that* pain.

"That's a ton of my money," Randall said, eyeing the envelope.

Miles ducked his head. "Yeah, and he was incredibly unappreciative!"

Randall stepped forward and touched Miles's shoulder, but Miles pulled away.

"Maybe he had a good reason, Miles."

"What reason? His only reason is that he's an ungrateful jerk!"

"Who's a jerk?" Tate had walked into the bathroom.

"You can't be in here," Randall said. "It's the men's bathroom."

"Who cares?" Tate put a hand on Miles's back, and he shrugged her off, too. "Whoa!" she said. "I'm only trying to help."

"Sorry," Miles said. "But he's such a stupid jerk!"

"He's your grandfather, Miles," Tate said. "Your grandpop."

"Doesn't matter." Miles paced in the small space, like a caged lion. "Bubbie Louise wouldn't ever in a million years have acted that way. Really, the present was supposed to be for *her*. I started saving all that time ago to buy the present for *her*. She's the one who really wanted to go there. But then she had to up and die!"

Miles collapsed into himself, collapsed into the truth of why this hurt so much. He sank to the floor with a defeated thud.

Randall and Tate flanked him and scrunched close.

"It's okay," Tate murmured.

"It's not," Miles cried, wiping his snotty nose on his sleeve. "And it's not going to be okay either, no matter what anyone says."

"You're right," Randall said. "It sucks."

It did suck. His bubbie was gone and his grandfather

was a jerk. Miles stood and wiped his eyes and nose with a few sheets of toilet paper. "I'm going home."

"Aw, man," Randall said. "You gotta stay for the rest of the party."

"No, I don't. I'm leaving."

Tate followed him out of the bathroom. "Then we're going with you. Right, Randall?"

"Um, sure."

Tate and Randall walked Miles the four blocks to his house, all of them hunched against the cold and no one talking.

They stopped in front of the steps to Miles's house. "Are you—?"

"I'm good," Miles said, even though he wasn't.

"So, we'll see you—"

"Yeah." Miles trudged up the steps and into his house.

Alone.

The Story Continues, Painfully

Even though Amy knew it would be only one more week of her dad being away, she felt a deep loneliness when he left Sunday night.

Uncle Matt wasn't home. He'd gone out with a friend.

Amy was alone in the house of death. She couldn't imagine why her dad thought this was a good idea.

Kat wasn't answering her texts. Tate wasn't either. Amy even texted Pam, hoping for a photo of Ernest or an update, but none arrived.

Sitting on her bed, Amy wrapped herself in the fuzzy purple blanket and wished for a few whispered words from her mom.

There were none.

She pulled out her notebook and purple pen and returned to her fictional friends.

Prince Harry returned to the tower room with a bowl of gruel each for Fiona and Lucky.

While it wasn't the tastiest thing they'd ever eaten, they were grateful for it.

Then the prince handed Fiona a loaf of crusty bread and a jar of water.

Fiona and Lucky finished every bite, every drop. Lucky burped to show his appreciation, then curled up in the corner of the cell and fell asleep.

"So, what is this idea of yours?" the prince asked, his green eyes ablaze with what Fiona figured must be hope.

She explained her idea and said that they could begin tomorrow, if the prince wanted.

The prince definitely wanted.

That night, before she fell into the deepest, most troubled sleep of her life, Fiona removed a few long, strong threads from the hem of her apron and set them aside, so she'd be ready for the morning.

The prince arrived early, with another jar of water for Fiona and Lucky and a cooked goose egg for each of them, along with herbs from the garden.

"The cook was in a fine mood this morning," Prince Harry declared. "And I'm ready to begin."

Fiona approached the prince and looked right into his enchanting eyes. "Before we do this, I want to be sure it's what you want. It will be painful. And, of course, temporary."

The prince returned Fiona's gaze with equal intensity. "This is exactly what I want. I couldn't be more sure. All this time, I assumed that when my mother told me to be exactly who I was, she meant who I was on the outside. That's why I never allowed anyone to remove my hair before. I now realize my mother meant to remain true to who I am on the inside. The outside—well, it's just the same as a book's cover—and I want to make a change to mine."

So they began the difficult job.

Fiona wrapped one of the threads from the hem of her apron around a few strands of the prince's hair and yanked.

"Ouch!" he screamed.

Fiona expected armed guards to rush in and impale her with spears, but of course she and the prince were so high up in the tower, no one could have heard him scream. "Are you all right?" Fiona asked. "Is it too painful?"

The prince's eyes watered. "Continue."

She did.

Every day, for a few hours, Fiona helped remove the prince's long hair. (He learned to tolerate the process without screaming.) And every day, the prince provided Fiona and Lucky with food, drink, companionship and a clean bucket for their waste.

What the prince didn't know—couldn't possibly know—was what Fiona did at night, after he had gone.

An Ending

Early Monday morning on lane 48, Miles and Randall laced up their bowling shoes, preparing to play a game before school.

"Want to lay down a few bucks on this one?" Randall asked.

"Nope."

Randall got up and staggered backward. "You don't want to play for money?" Randall put the back of his hand against Miles's forehead, but Miles slapped it away.

"Not sick. Just don't need the money anymore." Miles glared over at where his grandfather was sitting at his place at the counter. "Let's just bowl. Okay?"

"Okay."

Miles's angry bowling—using too much force and speed—cost him accuracy and points, but it made him feel a little better in the moment. He beat Randall by only a dozen points, which made him angry all over again. He should have crushed him.

As the boys walked away from the lane, Grandpop Billy rolled his chair into their path. "Miles, we need to talk."

"Maybe later," Miles said. "Don't want to be late for school."

"But . . ."

Miles darted around his grandfather's wheelchair and walked away without saying anything else.

Randall bumped into Miles's shoulder and gave him the side-eye. "What was that about?"

Miles kept walking.

The same thing happened the next three days.

Miles wished he didn't have to see his grandfather every day. It was hard to look at him after he'd been such a jerk.

On Friday, Miles's grandfather stopped him before the bowling began, before Randall even arrived.

"Sit," Billy insisted, pointing to a stool at the counter.

So Miles sat, but he wasn't happy about it.

"I need to explain why I couldn't take your gift."

Grandpop Billy waited until Miles turned to look at him. "Even though I really appreciate it."

Miles waited.

Grandpop Billy lifted his mug but then put it down without drinking. "You know your bubbie Louise wanted to go to the Bowling Hall of Fame. Right?"

Of course Miles knew. That was why he'd started saving for the gift in the first place.

"Well, what you might not know, Mr. Smarty Pants Silent Treatment, is that she'd been asking me to go there with her for years. For years!" Billy took a sip of coffee and slammed his mug down on the counter. "And being the stupid lunkhead I am, I told her we couldn't go because we had to be here at the lanes, that the place couldn't run without us." He sniffed hard and looked at Miles. "Isn't that the dumbest thing you ever heard?"

"Yes," Miles offered. "Mom and Dad could have taken care of everything."

"Thanks for nothing, kid." Grandpop Billy wiped his forehead. "I realize that now. Anyway, I always fig- ured there would be more time. Another tomorrow. And then . . ."

Miles finally felt bad for his grandfather. He reached out and patted the back of Pop's veiny hand. "That's why we should go together." Miles's eyes brightened. "You and me. In honor of Bubbie Louise. It's supposed to be an amazing place. There are exhibits about five thousand years of bowling history. Five thousand years! And I'll help you during the plane ride and—"

"No way, bud. Wouldn't feel right. I won't go to that place without your bubbie."

"Well, then I guess you'll never go." Miles knew it was a mean thing to say, but he couldn't help himself.

Billy put his hand on top of Miles's. "You spend that money on something else. Something good. Something important that will matter to someone."

Miles pulled his hand away. "I thought that's what I was doing." He grabbed his stuff and stomped off to intercept Randall at the door and head to school.

He didn't feel like bowling this morning.

• • •

Two weeks later, Miles's mom, behind the front counter at the bowling center, said to him, "You really ought to make up with your grandpop."

"I know. I will," Miles said. "But I'm not ready yet."

"Miles . . ."

"What?"

His mom leaned close and pressed her forehead against his, then pulled away and started organizing shoes in the slots behind the counter. "Your grandfather said something strange to me last night."

"What?"

She stopped straightening shoes. "Well, he said Bubbie Louise had been calling to him."

"She'd been what?" Miles's heart sped up, and a familiar panic set in. "What'd you say to him?"

"I told him not to answer!"

"Do you think that means—?"

"I don't know what it means. But I do know you should make up with your grandfather. He wasn't try- ing to make you feel bad, Miles."

"But he did."

Miles's mom put her arm around his shoulders and squeezed. Then she kissed him on top of his head. "Just talk to him, Miles."

"I will."

But he didn't.

Four days later, Billy Spagoski answered Louise's call.

He died in his sleep.

No. No. No. No. No.

Tate and Amy walked into the library together, Tate wearing her knit penguin hat and Amy wearing a purple knit monkey hat—a gift from Tate.

"How are my two favorite library volunteers today?" Mr. Schu asked.

"Awesome sauce." Tate flexed her biceps and struck a bodybuilding pose.

"Come on, Wonder Woman." Amy pushed Tate toward the back, where a cart of books was waiting for them.

The girls were halfway through the top shelf when Tate looked at her phone. "Oh no!"

"What?" Amy asked.

Tate shook her head. "No. No. No. No. No."

"What? What? What? What? What?"

Tate looked at Amy. "Miles's grandfather died."

Amy pictured the older man at the end of the snack counter at Buckington Bowl. "Huh?"

"And Miles never . . ." Tate shook her head. "I've got to go."

Tate hurried to the circulation desk, and Amy followed.

"Mr. Schu, I need a pass to go to the nurse. Like, now."

He handed it to her.

Amy watched her friend rush from the library. She felt hollowed out, but she wasn't sure why. She hadn't even really known Miles's grandfather.

"Are *you* okay, Amy?" Mr. Schu asked.

Was she? Amy nodded even though she wasn't sure. She trudged back to the cart and continued shelving books. But the sad news about Miles's grandfather kept her from concentrating on what she was doing. The stickers on the books weren't making sense anymore. Book titles blurred. Memories—painful memories of her mom's illness—seeped in.

This time, even books couldn't save Amy from the tidal wave of pain crashing over her, flooding through her and ultimately leaking from her eyes in a stream of sadness.

Mr. Schu was standing by with a gentle pat on the back, a handful of tissues and some warm words. "Is there anything I can do?"

Amy shook her head.

"Maybe you'd better go to the nurse, too." Mr. Schu handed her a pass, and she walked to the office of the nurse she'd met the first day of school. This time the problem wasn't on the outside of Amy's head, but inside. And inside her heart, too.

Not long after, her dad came to pick her up.

"What's wrong, Ames?"

A fresh flow of tears started, and she buried herself against her dad's strong chest.

He got her to the car, then back to Eternal Peace, where he held her and cried along with her. They eventually talked about her mom. And he told her the funeral for Miles's grandfather would take place at Eternal Peace.

Amy said she couldn't go to that funeral.

"It's up to you, Amy," her dad said. "I won't ask you to go. I know it will be hard."

"Too hard," she whispered, then swiped an arm across her runny nose.

"I know." He held her even more tightly. "I know."

Then, like a feather floating on a wisp of wintery wind, Amy's mom's voice whispered in her mind: *You must go to the funeral, sweets. That boy will need you there.*

That was when Amy knew that if she was any kind of friend at all, she'd be there.

For Miles.

Amy thought of the people who came to her mom's funeral to support her and her dad, and she understood. Sometimes we do hard things not for ourselves, but to make things easier for someone else.

That's right, sweets.

A Sad Truth

Here, Dear Reader, comes the part of the story where a sad truth is revealed.

When you lose someone you love—someone who is the very foundation of your being—the pain from that loss never fully goes away. It does something sneaky: It hibernates inside you, like a sleeping bear waiting to be awakened by spring. Except instead of waiting for spring, the pain from a deep loss waits for someone else's loss to awaken it.

Then it roars to life, like a wild, aching beast.

That's what happened to Amy. Miles's loss awakened her own. The intense pain from losing her mom arose from its deep slumber inside her and roared its terrible roar.

It happens to all of us, Dear Reader.

And for that, I'm so sorry.

The Beginning of the Worst Day

Miles woke after barely sleeping and didn't want to shower, didn't want to get dressed. He felt like he was reliving Bubbie Louise's funeral. Then he thought about how hard this must be for his parents, so he forced himself to walk downstairs to the kitchen.

His mom and dad were at the table, mugs of coffee before them, but they weren't lifting the mugs to their lips.

Miles took a seat.

Then Mercedes, her hair wet, walked in and grabbed a banana. Before sitting, she hugged her mom and dad. Then she hugged Miles.

It felt good, but Miles knew he didn't deserve it because of how awful he'd been to his grandfather before he died.

A tiny voice in his head told him he might be partly responsible for his grandfather's death. Might have upset Grandpop so much it affected his weak heart. Miles's rational, logical mind knew this wasn't true, that it wasn't his fault at all. He knew his grandfather hadn't been well for a long time.

Still, he couldn't get that tiny voice in his head to shut up.

The Funeral

The people sitting in the chairs at Eternal Peace in the room with the white casket were pretty much the same people who'd been sitting at the bowling center for Billy Spagoski's seventy-fifth-birthday party a few weeks before.

Life and death had a way of mixing together sometimes.

Miles didn't like when the minister talked about his grandfather, because it was a stranger talking about the man Miles had known his whole life. He felt better when Stick rolled up to the front of the room, tears streaming down his cheeks, and talked about how Miles's grandfather gave him the money to start the tailoring shop that he owned to that day. Miles felt better when his dad got up there and blubbered about what a great father Billy had been to him and Miles's mom and what a terrific grandfather he'd been to Miles and Mercedes. That last part made Miles cry extra hard because he hadn't been such a terrific grandson.

Then it was time for the family to say goodbye, which meant they'd walk to the casket, look at Grandpop Billy's body and say their final words.

Miles knew exactly what he needed to say, but he didn't want anyone else to hear.

His dad took his hand and held on with an iron grip, a grip that might have meant *I'm still here, son*.

Miles and his dad stood in front of the casket together, after his mom and sister had had their turn.

"I'm gonna miss you, Pop," George Spagoski said. Then he kissed his fingers and touched his father's forehead.

Miles wouldn't do that. He knew what was inside the body in the coffin. He knew the body looked like his grandpop but wasn't really him. But Miles also figured his grandpop's spirit was nearby, so he'd say what he had to and hope he heard it.

The people from the funeral home had laid a photo on Pop's chest, tucked under his crossed arms. It was the photo of him and Bubbie Louise that had hung in the center of the "Greatest Stories Ever Bowled" bulletin board. Miles even saw the tiny hole from the pushpin. He didn't want an empty space in the center of that board, but he knew it would match the empty space in the center of himself.

He took a shaky breath and spoke in a whisper. "Pop? I'm sorry I was mean to you. I'm sorry I didn't forgive you. But I do now." He gulped. "And I hope you can forgive me. I love you, Pop. You have to know how much I love you."

Miles's dad wrapped a strong arm around his shoulders and whispered in his ear, "He knows, son. He knows."

At that moment, they both looked down at Billy Spagoski lying in the silk-lined white casket and plunged into waterfalls of despair.

Amy, at the Funeral

Amy had been hanging back, standing at the rear of the room where the funeral was taking place, in case she felt the need to flee. She knew her mom wanted her there, but Amy wasn't sure she could do it. So far, she'd been able to stay and watch. So far. But then both Miles and his dad burst out crying at the same time.

Amy froze. Should she go up to Miles? His dad? What would she say? What *could* she say? That everything would be okay? She knew better than most it wasn't true.

That's when her dad, dressed in a navy-blue suit, swooped in, put a strong arm around Miles's shoulders and pulled him over for a hug and a few quiet, reassuring words at the same time that Uncle Matt put a hand on Miles's dad's back and guided him away to offer gentle words of support, too.

Amy felt awful for spying on this tender scene, but she couldn't pull herself away.

She couldn't believe what she was witnessing. Her dad with Miles. Uncle Matt with Miles's dad. It was like magic, the way they spoke and comforted them. The way Miles and his dad softened, relaxed and stopped sobbing. The way they both nodded, like they were taking in the words of comfort and using them to heal themselves.

Amy remembered how her dad had comforted people when he was a Unitarian Universalist minister back in Chicago. She remembered the kind words he said at the end of his sermons: "If you're looking for peace, may this be your sanctuary. If you're looking for social justice, may we work together as a committed community. If you're looking for a home, may we be your family." Back then, her dad's words filled her up, and she could see people in the congregation smiling and nodding. Amy realized her dad was really good at this, the way she was good at writing.

Something cracked wide open inside Amy. Her dad had taken a broken person and helped repair him, helped his heart begin to heal. She knew Miles's heart would break again and again and need to be healed many times, just like Amy's had and would. But her dad—*her dad!*—had done this impossible thing. Amy finally understood why he wanted to work at Eternal Peace Funeral Home—not that he *had* to work there, but that he *wanted* to. He had the ability to help people feel less broken on their worst days. And that, Amy knew, was no small thing.

This simple understanding made a difference in the way Amy thought about where she was living. It shone light into the darkness.

Amy sniffed, and Miles turned his head toward her.

She smiled warmly at him.

He nodded at her and smiled sadly.

Amy was glad she'd been there for her friend, even if it was only to offer a smile. Sometimes that was enough to matter.

And Amy felt so proud of her dad and the work he did.

She was glad she'd decided to go to the funeral.

Thanks, Mom.

FRAME NINE

How Life Goes On

FRAME 6   FRAME 10

FRAME 6   FRAME 10

FRAME 6   FRAME 10

FRAME 6   FRAME 7   FRAME 8   FRAME 9   FRAME 10

FRAME 6   FRAME 7   FRAME 8   FRAME 9   FRAME 10

FRAME 6   FRAME 7   FRAME 8   FRAME 9   FRAME 10

Shut Up and Bowl

Miles missed a few days of school.

On the day he'd planned to go back, Randall showed up outside the automatic doors, right on time, smudging up the glass. This time, Miles didn't have the energy to get the Windex and clean it off. *What does it matter anyway?*

The whole bowling center was dark and cold and quiet.

The boys sat on stools at the snack counter.

"It's weird sitting here without him," Randall said.

Miles looked at the empty stool where his grandpop always sat. He looked at the empty space in the center of the bulletin board. "Yeah." *They're both gone now.*

"You doing okay, man?"

Miles slumped. He shook his head.

Randall put a palm on his back. "Sorry."

Miles sniffed. "I keep thinking I'm doing better, but then it'll hit me all over again, like a bowling ball to the gut."

"That sucks."

"You know what he said a few days after I gave him that gift?" Miles asked.

Randall shook his head.

"He said I should spend the money on something good. Something important that would matter to someone."

Randall's eyes brightened. "You could give some of it back to me. It's kind of mine anyway."

Miles glared.

"Yeah. So what were you thinking?"

"No clue. I've saved up for the trip to the Bowling Hall of Fame for so long, I can't imagine using the money for anything else."

"But your grandpop wanted you to. Right?"

"I guess."

"What about buying tickets to the school dance so me and Tate and you and Amy could all go together?"

"I don't think that's what Pop had in mind. Plus, the amount is way more money than those tickets cost."

"Don't rub it in."

"Well, quit talking about the dumb dance."

Randall put his hands up. "Yeah, sure. Sorry."

"It's okay. I'm sorry." Miles ran his hand through his hair. "Hey, you want to bowl?"

"I do."

They hopped down from their stools.

"Just so you know, I'm probably going to kick your butt today, Spagoski. I've been working on my form."

"Sure you are, Rand. You and what army of pro bowlers?"

"Seriously, I've got my bowling mojo going today."

"Yeah, whatever you need to believe."

Randall snapped the tips of his shirt collar. "Oh, you'll see."

While they were putting on their bowling shoes, Miles said, "Did I ever tell you about the guy from West Palm Beach, Florida, who died from eating too many cockroaches?"

"What? No! That's gross!"

"Yeah, it was some kind of bug-eating contest at a pet store. The guy won, but then he vomited and choked to death. His girlfriend was with him. She called 911, but they couldn't save him."

"The bug-eating dude had a girlfriend?" Randall raised his eyebrows.

"Yeah," Miles said. "Guess there really is someone

for everybody." He briefly thought of Amy. "Want to know the official cause of death?"

"No!"

"Accidental choking on arthropod body parts."

"Spagoski?"

"Yeah, Rand?"

"Shut up and bowl."

So he did.

It was the first game Miles had bowled since his grandfather died. And it was a good thing Randall hadn't placed a bet on the game, because Miles beat him by fifty-seven beautiful points.

But a perfect game still eluded him.

There is a crack in everything. That's how the light gets in.

—Leonard Cohen

Talking in the Library

"I feel terrible for Miles," Tate said as she put the graphic novel *Smile* on a shelf.

"Yeah. Me too." Amy shelved *Yummy: The Last Days of a Southside Shorty*. "He must be so sad. I wish there were a way to cheer him up."

"Well . . ." Tate twirled a bit of blue hair around her index finger. "We could talk him into coming to the party at my house the night before the school dance."

"Do you think he'll come to your party?" Amy hoped he would.

Tate filled her cheek with air and let it out slowly. "Randall told me Miles doesn't leave his house or the lanes, except for school. He's really upset."

Amy understood how he felt. "You talk to Randall a lot?"

"Sure, we're neighbors. Remember?"

"I mean . . . you know."

"Yeah." Tate ducked her head. "He calls me some nights. Told me he had to sit in his closet so his brothers and sisters didn't bother him. One time, I fell asleep while he was talking and woke up like five minutes later and he was still at it."

"That's hilarious," Amy said.

"He's definitely a future lawyer," Tate said.

"He already dresses like one," Amy said, thinking of his stylish clothes. "Even his jeans have sharp creases in them."

"Oh, you should have seen him in his bow tie days. He wore one every single day of fifth grade. Ooh-la-la!"

Both girls cracked up.

"Hey!" Mr. Schu called back to them. "Are you girls shelving or chatting?"

"We're chatting," Tate replied.

"Yes, absolutely chatting," Amy echoed.

"In that case . . ." Mr. Schu saluted them. "Carry on, young pages!"

So they did.

When You Love Someone . . .

Mercedes texted Miles late one evening.

How you doing, Miles?

OK. You?

I miss Pop. You?

Yeah. 😞

Then Miles didn't text anything for a while. He wasn't sure what to say to his sister, so he held the phone and waited to see if she'd write anything else.

Hey, how's that nice girl doing?

Amy?

Yeah.

How should I know?

Miles! Don't you ever see her?

He bit his bottom lip, deciding whether he should tell his sister the truth.

I haven't left the house or the lanes.
Don't want to leave Mom and Dad alone.

Oh, Miles.

He didn't want his sister's pity.

Going to bed now.

G'night Miles. Love you.

Miles made sure he told the people who mattered to him that he loved them. Just in case.

Love you, too, Mercedes. <3

Aw. You're the best brother.

Yeah. I know. ;)

Miles turned off his phone and lay in bed, recalling how his grandfather had looked in the casket. He remembered what he hadn't said to Pop before he died. Miles ached to have one more day to tell his grandfather those things, to hear Pop's voice saying that he forgave him and that he loved him.

Friends Being Friends

Randall, Tate and Amy walked into Buckington Bowl after school.

"Hey there, Mrs. Spagoski," Randall said to Miles's mom.

"Oh, hi, guys." Miles's mom came out from behind the counter and hugged each of them. "I'm so glad you're here. Miles could sure use his friends."

The trio walked along the worn carpet, where a woman was measuring.

"New carpet going in?" Randall asked Miles when they reached the snack counter.

"Yup," Miles said. "Dad's finally making some of those improvements he's wanted to."

There was a heaviness in the air surrounding that statement.

"I kind of like this carpet," Randall said. "Used to it after all these years."

"Yeah, me too," Miles said.

"Hey there." Tate gave Miles a hug.

"What can I get you guys?" Miles's dad asked, knocking two knuckles on the counter.

"Nothing," Randall said.

"Nothing for me either," Amy said.

"Loaded fries," Tate said. "And a vanilla milk shake, please."

Randall and Amy glared at her.

"What? I worked out really hard this morning. I'm hungry."

"Okay then," Randall said. "Guess I'll take a burger and fries."

"Hot chocolate, please," Amy added.

Miles ate and drank nothing. Not even a sip of his usual root beer.

"Um, Miles," Amy said, "how close have you ever come to bowling a perfect game?"

Miles perked up, but before he could answer, his dad called from the back, "He bowled a two eighty-nine once. One of the proudest days of my life."

Miles ducked his head. "Yeah, I thought I was going to finally do it—bowl my first perfect game—but I choked on the last frame. Maybe I should have walked away before I played that frame, like the lady who never completed her three-game series." He looked toward the "Greatest Stories Ever Bowled" bulletin board, but the empty place in the middle hurt his heart, so he looked down.

"Hey, two eighty-nine is amazing," Amy said. "I've never even broken a hundred."

Randall laughed.

Tate punched him.

"Ouch! What?"

Tate shook her head.

After they ate, the trio talked Miles into bowling one game with them.

Miles's heart wasn't in it. He noticed again how Amy was off-balance when she wore bowling shoes, how she rubbed her left hip near the end of the game.

And he wondered why nothing could ever be easy.

Preparing

Amy didn't say it out loud, but when her dad dropped her off at Tate's place, she hoped Miles would be there. The more she hung out with him, the more she liked him. Plus now, sadly, they had something in common—losing someone they loved.

But he wasn't there.

Of course, no one outside of Tate's family was at the bed-and-breakfast yet, since Tate had asked Amy to come an hour early to help set up for the party. And Tate's parents hadn't booked any guests for the night so she could have the whole place to herself with her friends.

In her bedroom, Tate squealed. "Check it out!" And she showed off the blue dress draped over her bed.

Marmalade walked right across the dress.

"Marmalade!" Tate shrieked. She picked the cat up and put her on the floor. "What do you think, Amy? This is the consignment shop find I told you about, combined with some fancy-pants stitchery I did." Tate smoothed the dress with her palm. "Just before you came, I sent Perla a photo, and she said it would definitely have been blog-worthy if we had ever created that fashion blog we'd talked about. What do you think? I totally have to bring my A-game to compete with Randall's style. Right?"

Amy ran her fingers over the silky dress and wished, wished, wished she had a dress at home laid out on her bed. Wished she were going to the dance tomorrow night. Wished she had a date to take her and a mom to fuss over her before she left—taking photos and kissing her cheek, creating a lipstick smudge that she'd rub off with her thumb. "It's beautiful." Amy cleared her throat. "Randall will think it's awesome."

Tate squealed again. "Thanks." She hugged Amy tightly. "I wish you were going, too."

Amy shrugged as though it was no big deal, but she couldn't help feeling like she was in the pages of Cinderella's story. Tate's sparkling pink nail polish distracted her. "You have the coolest nail polish colors."

Tate wiggled her fingers. "It's from a line of nail

polish called Wild Expressions. They have the best names for the different colors. This shade is called 'The Color Your Cheeks Get When You See a Boy You Like.'"

Amy laughed at the name, and it felt good.

"Hey," Tate said. "Why don't we get ready for this party?"

Amy nodded. "Let's do it." She was glad to have something to do to keep her from feeling sorry for herself.

When they left Tate's bedroom, Marmalade pranced out after them.

"Oh no you don't." Tate scooped up her cat, put her back in the bedroom and shut the door. "Randall's allergic to you, little miss, so you'll be spending the party in there."

Marmalade meowed through the door in reply.

Tate and Amy got snacks ready, picked out music and waited for the boys to arrive.

But only one boy arrived.

"Let's Go!"

Back at Buckington Bowl, Miles was slumped over the snack counter, ice melting in an untouched glass of root beer.

He looked behind him at the new carpet, sleek black with white flecks that glowed when the lights were low. He hated it, and he knew his grandpop would have hated it, too. Miles wished his dad had waited a little longer before making the changes Pop hadn't wanted.

"How you doing, champ?" Miles's dad swiped a towel across the counter.

"Lousy."

"I can see that. Would a fresh root beer help?"

Miles looked past his root beer at the empty stool across the counter. "Nope."

"With a scoop of vanilla ice cream in it?"

"I said NO!"

"Okay." Miles's dad held up his hands. "You don't have to take it out on me." He walked back into the kitchen.

Miles was glad his dad had left. He wanted to be by himself. But he also didn't want to be alone. It didn't make any sense, but so little had, lately.

Miles's mom slipped onto the stool next to him. "I have only a minute because we're pretty full tonight."

Miles looked around. There were about ten lanes being used. "That's full?"

She shrugged. "For us it is."

Miles put his head in his hands.

"Come on, bud. Please buck up."

"I don't want to buck up," Miles mumbled.

"What are your friends doing tonight? Maybe you could invite them over to bowl a few games."

Without lifting his head, Miles said, "Tate's having a party."

"Party? What kind of party?"

Miles was sorry he'd said anything. "Just a party for Randall, her and Amy."

"And you?" his mom asked.

"Well, Tate asked me to come, but—"

"Get your coat."

Miles lifted his head. "Huh?"

"Never mind. I'll get it for you." Then she yelled toward the kitchen, "Sweetheart, I'm driving Miles to Tate's house. Say so long."

"So long, Miles!"

"And please keep an eye on the front counter until I get back."

"Will do," he called. "I'll be right there."

"But—" Miles started.

"But nothing," his mom said. "Let's go!"

Once she'd grabbed his coat, Miles's mom whisked him away from Buckington Bowl into the bright-orange van with the giant fake bowling pins and bowling ball on top. She drove like a firefighter heading toward a three-alarm blaze.

When they screeched up to Buckington Bed & Breakfast, Miles's mom practically shoved him out of the car. "Have fun with your friends!"

And she zoomed off.

Breath

"**M**iles! You're here!" Tate yanked him into the living room.

She pulled Miles's arm so hard it hurt, but he didn't say anything. Just stood there.

"My man!" Randall slapped Miles hard on the back. "Glad you're here. Now, drink some orange soda."

"What? Why? I'm not thirsty."

Randall thrust a paper cup of orange soda into Miles's hand. "Yes, you are." Then he walked off.

Miles preferred root beer, but orange was okay, so he took a sip. Then he realized Amy was standing off to the side.

"Hey, Miles," she said. "I'm really glad you made it." She was smiling. It reminded Miles of how Amy was there at his grandpop's funeral, how she'd smiled at him when he needed it most.

A flow of energy Miles hadn't felt in a long time surged through him. It felt like shrugging off a heavy winter coat because the sun was shining and spring had arrived. Miles looked around the room at his old friends and his new friend. Music was playing. The room was brightly lit. There was a cup of soda in his hand. He wouldn't have told her so, but Miles was glad his mom had driven him to the party. He belonged here. "Hey, Amy," he finally said.

Randall skidded over and nodded toward Miles's cup. "Drink up, my man!" As if to show Miles how to do it, Randall chugged the orange soda from his own cup.

Miles slurped some more soda, but his stomach wasn't feeling terrific, so he put the cup down.

That was when Randall grabbed Miles's elbow. "We'll be right back," he said to Amy and Tate. He led Miles into the kitchen.

There, Randall backed Miles up to the fridge, got right in his face and whispered fiercely, "When the soda bottle is empty, we're going to use it to play spin the bottle." Deep, rattling wheezes punctuated Randall's words. "So drink the soda—now."

"Hey, your wheezing sounds pretty bad, Rand."

"I'm good," Randall said. "Tate put her cat in the bedroom and vacuumed the rug in the living room."

"But even so, it sounds—"

"I'm good." Randall patted the pocket where he kept his inhaler. "Now drink the soda. Okay?"

"Okay. Okay." Miles was glad to be there, but he didn't feel like drinking any more soda.

• • •

Somehow, Amy ended up sitting in a big chair with Miles. Tate was on the couch next to Randall. Really close to him.

"Where are your parents?" Miles asked.

"Back bedroom," Tate said, moving a smidge closer to Randall.

Miles did not move closer to Amy. In fact, the chair they were sitting on felt a little claustrophobic. He thought about telling Amy the true story of a forty-five-year-old man in Brazil who was crushed to death by a cow that climbed onto his roof from a nearby hillside, then fell through the roof on top of the man asleep in his bed. Miles thought Amy would especially appreciate the last part of the story: the man's wife, who'd been sleeping next to him, and the cow were both unharmed. But Miles wasn't sure this party was the right place to share the story. So instead he said,

"Seems like you and Tate have become really good friends."

Amy nodded.

Miles waited for her to say something more, but when she didn't, he took another swig of orange soda, even though his stomach was feeling full and sort of cranky.

Finally, Amy said, "Today, Tate showed me the dress she worked on for the dance. It's really nice."

The dance. That stupid school dance. Miles had forgotten about it, especially after what happened to Pop. If Miles hadn't cared about the dance before, he cared even less about it now, if that was even possible. Then Miles looked at Amy. Really looked at her. She seemed eager, like she was waiting for him to say something. He remembered Randall telling him he should ask Amy to the dance. "Do you, um, like to dance?"

"Oh yeah," Amy said. "I do."

Miles wanted to say *Me too,* but the truth was, he didn't. He liked to bowl. He wished the school would hold a bowl-a-thon instead of a dumb dance. And if they held it at Buckington Bowl, it would help business, too.

"Do you?" Amy asked.

Miles shook his head. He couldn't lie to her.

"Oh."

Amy looked disappointed.

Miles's heart was so hurt, he couldn't stand seeing someone else hurting. So he blurted words that tripped over each other. "But maybe if you want to, um, we could . . . you know, go together. I mean, if it's not too late for us to, I mean, get tickets and all." Miles knew he said everything wrong, so he was surprised when Amy looked happier. Much happier.

"Well, it's about time, Miles Spagoski!" Tate screamed.

Miles gulped down the rest of the soda in his paper cup.

"Well, look at that," Randall said, then sucked in a raspy breath. "Miles finally manned up about the dance and . . . and . . . Hey, the soda bottle's practically empty."

"Oh yes it is," Tate said. "But you know, we didn't have to do it the old-fashioned way." She held up her phone. "I have a cool spin-the-bottle app."

"Now you tell me." Randall laughed, but the laugh turned into a cough.

"You okay?" Tate asked.

Randall nodded.

"Okay, then." Tate dove to the rug in the middle of the living room. "Come on, everyone!"

"Yeah." Randall grabbed the nearly empty bottle

and swigged the last of the soda. He let out a gross burp. "Let's . . . get this . . . party started."

Miles thought Randall's wheezing sounded worse, but he didn't want to say anything in front of the girls. He had a feeling Randall would just get mad at him if he did, so he got up out of the chair and offered Amy his hand; but she got up by herself.

They joined Tate and Randall on the living room rug, creating a circle.

"I guess I'll go first," Tate said. "Since it's my house and all."

"Okay." Amy bit her thumbnail.

"Fine with me," Miles said. He pretended he wasn't nervous. But he hoped the bottle didn't land on him, because he didn't want to have to kiss Tate. She was cute, but only a friend. He might like kissing Amy, but it would be awkward in front of everybody. What if he messed up? His stomach was all in burbles and refused to calm down.

Randall, up on his knees and leaning forward, said nothing, but a rattling wheeze escaped his lips at regular intervals.

Miles wished Randall would take a couple puffs from his inhaler to quiet the wheezing.

Tate managed to spin the empty bottle so that it pointed at Randall.

Tate and Randall leaned toward each other, closed their eyes and kissed.

"Your turn," Randall said, passing the bottle to Miles. "Now, don't make it . . . land on . . . me." There was a deep, whistling wheeze coming from Randall. "Or Tate!"

Miles's stomach roiled and made a gurgling noise he hoped no one else heard. He gave the bottle a weak spin. It landed to the side of Amy.

"Close enough," Tate said, readjusting the bottle so it pointed directly at Amy.

"Tate!" Amy said.

"What? I was just fixing it. It would have landed on you completely, but the carpet fibers got in the way."

"Carpet fibers?" Amy asked.

"Maybe you should mow your rug," Miles said to Tate.

Randall laughed, then started coughing. And coughing.

"You okay?" Miles asked.

Randall waved his words away. "Come on," he said between coughs. "You're . . . not . . . getting out of this."

Miles and Amy got up on their knees, like Tate and Randall had done.

The roiling in Miles's stomach intensified. It crept

up out of his stomach and inched its way toward his throat. *Better get this over with quick,* Miles thought, *before my stomach makes another embarrassing noise.* And he leaned forward.

Amy leaned forward, too, parted her lips and closed her eyes.

But they moved together too quickly and their foreheads bumped.

Miles leaned back and smiled at Amy. He thought of when his bowling shoe hit her and made a mark at that very spot on her forehead. Then he leaned in and kissed her—his lips pressed gently against her soft lips.

When Miles pulled back, Amy touched her fingers to her lips.

Miles wondered if it was Amy's first kiss, like it was his. Then he turned his head just in time for a Vesuvius-sized burp to erupt from his mouth.

"Ew!" Tate yelled. "That was gross!"

"Sorry," Miles said, grateful he hadn't burped in Amy's face. "It's Randall's fault for making me drink all that soda."

Randall would have responded, but he was too busy falling over laughing at Miles.

"Jerk," Miles muttered.

But then he saw Randall bolt up straight, his eyes bugging out.

"Randall?" Tate asked.

Randall didn't answer. He reached into his pocket.

"My God," Miles said, realizing what was happening. "You okay, Rand?"

Randall nodded. He had his hand on his inhaler. He gave it a weak shake, pulled off the cap, depressed the device and breathed in. Another shake. Another inhale. Shake. Shake. Press. Press. Shake. Press.

"Rand?" Miles said, his heart hammering.

Randall looked at Miles with complete panic in his eyes and mouthed: *Empty*.

Miles couldn't believe how pale Randall's lips were.

Then Randall made a small, strangled sound and crumpled onto the rug. He breathed in fast, tiny gasps, like he was trying to get air through a clogged miniature drinking straw.

Miles couldn't move. Couldn't speak. The worst thing that could happen was happening in front of him. And he couldn't do anything but watch.

"Mom! Dad!" Tate screamed, and ran from the room.

Amy had her phone out and had already dialed 911. She spoke fast: ". . . medical emergency at Buckington Bed and Breakfast. My friend . . . he's . . . not breathing!"

Miles still couldn't move. Could barely breathe himself.

Randall lay motionless on the floor. He wasn't even making tiny gasping sounds now.

Tate's parents rushed in and crouched beside Randall while Amy kept talking to the 911 dispatcher.

Tate shook and pressed Randall's inhaler, trying to get it to work. "It's my fault. I should have vacuumed better. I should have—"

"Not your fault," her dad said. "Run next door and get his parents. Hurry, Tate!"

Tate hurried.

Amy chewed her thumbnail.

Miles backed up a few steps, shaking his head.

In no time, Randall's mom burst in. She waved something orange. "I've got an extra inhaler. Make way." She knelt on the floor beside her son, trying to get the medicine into him. "Breathe, Randall!" she screamed. "Breathe!"

Miles bit his bottom lip so hard, he tasted blood. *Please don't die, Randall. Please don't. Please . . .*

A siren wailed. Paramedics rushed into the living room.

They worked on Randall, got him onto a stretcher and then whisked him off in the ambulance, its siren screaming through the dark night.

Once Randall and his mom were gone, it was too quiet in the living room.

Deathly quiet.

Except for a single, long meow from Marmalade, who was still shut inside Tate's bedroom.

After

Miles, Tate and Amy sat in the living room, where, only an hour and a half earlier, the worst thing that had happened was Miles's massive burp, which Randall had thought was hilarious.

Now the three of them wiped leaky eyes and noses and wondered, worried about their friend. And absolutely nothing was hilarious.

"It's my fault," Tate said for what seemed like the millionth time.

"It's not," Miles insisted.

"I knew he was allergic to Marmalade. I shouldn't have had the party at my house."

"But you put Marmalade away," Amy said. "And vacuumed."

"Still," Tate said, her shoulders slumping. "It wasn't enough." She pounded her forehead with her fist.

"Stop." Miles gently touched her wrist. "It was my burp that made him laugh and that caused him to . . . to . . ." Miles shook his head. "Sometimes things just happen."

Amy nodded and patted Tate's back. "It's not anyone's fault."

Tate's dad carried in a tray with hot chocolate for everyone. "I'm sure Randall will be okay."

But Amy knew that wasn't always the case.

"If he's still in the hospital tomorrow," Tate's dad said, "maybe you guys can visit him and cheer him up."

"Tomorrow?" Tate whispered.

"Yes, tomorrow," her dad said. "I can drive you all over, if you'd like."

Tate's eyes got wide. "Tomorrow's the dance."

"The dance," Amy muttered.

"The dance," Miles echoed.

FRAME TEN

A Funny Thing Happened on the Way to Happily-Ever-After

Not at the Dance

The next evening, while many of the students and faculty from Buckington Middle School were dressed in their fanciest attire and were dancing under shimmering rainbow lights at the Eagleton Country Club on Route 309 in Doylesburg—the town over from Buckington—three friends were jammed together near their buddy's hospital bed in a room that smelled like overcooked chicken, industrial-strength cleaning fluid and hand sanitizer.

There were plastic tubes in Randall's nostrils, and the tubes were attached to a longer tube that delivered oxygen.

Randall lifted his fingers off the white sheet that covered his body and wiggled them toward his friends.

"You really scared us, Randall." Tate crossed her arms over her chest.

Miles stared and didn't say anything. It felt like he was looking at a ghost. He'd been so sure Randall was going to die last night that his mind was having trouble processing the fact that his friend was lying there, alive.

Maybe, Miles thought, he didn't need to worry about death and dying every minute of every day. Maybe his worrying didn't actually keep terrible things from happening. Maybe it just made him miserable.

Randall's mom rushed in and gave each of the friends a hug. "You kids did such a good job calling for help and running to get me." She wiped tears from her cheeks. "Randall's father and I are so grateful."

Amy and Tate nodded.

Miles felt like a traitor because he knew he'd done absolutely nothing to help his friend at his worst moment. If Amy and Tate hadn't been there, Randall probably wouldn't be here now. Standing beside his friend's hospital bed, Miles promised himself he'd never freeze up like that again. He'd never stand by when someone needed his help. No matter how scared he was.

"You saved his life, you know," Randall's mom told them.

Tate waved away the remark.

"No, you did. Asthma is serious stuff, and attacks can come on quickly."

Randall mumbled something.

"Huh?" his mom asked. "What's that, baby guy?"

"The dance," Randall said. He was looking at Tate. "I'm sorry about ruining the dance for you."

Tate took Randall's fingers with one hand and wiped tears away with the other. "I'm just glad you're still here, you idiot. I don't care about the stupid dance."

Everyone laughed. Then Miles looked at Amy. He wondered if *she* cared about the stupid dance. He had a feeling she did.

"I'm going to the cafeteria to get everyone some ice cream," Randall's mom said. "That's what we all need now. Some Neapolitan ice cream cups." She grabbed her purse and left.

Randall smiled at Tate. "I'll make it up to you." He squeezed her fingers.

Tate sniffed. "Really, Rand. It doesn't matter."

"It matters," Randall said.

Miles knew the dance mattered to each of his friends for different reasons. Even if it didn't matter to him, it mattered to them. And *they* mattered to him.

That's when an idea popped into Miles's mind.

"What are you so happy about?" Randall asked.

Miles hadn't realized he was grinning.

The Idea

Back home, Miles could think of nothing but his new idea.

He spent the rest of the night on his computer, figuring things out, ordering items. He made lists and checked them twice, then checked them again. Then once more. He texted Mercedes to ask her some stuff.

That night, for the first time in a really long time, Miles Spagoski didn't lie in bed worrying about death. He fell right to sleep.

The next evening, at the lanes, Miles had something important to ask his parents.

And Stick.

Afterward, he went over and sat on his grandfather's stool for the first time ever.

Things at Buckington Bowl looked different from that angle.

Miles tried to imagine what his grandfather must have thought about, all those years ago, when Bubbie Louise walked into the bowling center with her girlfriends and sat on the stool across the counter from him. Miles wondered if the feeling was similar to how he felt the first time Amy showed up at the lanes . . . and he spilled his soda on her.

Miles glanced at the empty spot in the center of the "Greatest Stories Ever Bowled" bulletin board. He inhaled sharply, thinking of where that photo was now—resting on his pop's cold chest in a casket buried in the ground.

Miles patted the edge of the stool beneath him. "Thank you, Pop," he whispered. "I think you'd be real proud of how I decided to spend the money."

Then he slipped off the stool and got back to work on his idea.

The First Happily-Ever-After

What happened to Randall wore Amy out emotionally. It reminded her too much of some of the things that happened to her mom after she got sick and the cancer spread. The ambulance. The hospital stays. The tubes in Randall's nose looked like the ones her mom had needed near the end. It was all too much, so Amy spent a lot of time at Eternal Peace Funeral Home in her room, wrapped in her fuzzy blanket, clutching her trusty notebook and purple pen.

And she wrote.

Fiona had been stashing all of Prince Harry's hair under a big loose stone in her prison cell. Every night after Prince

Harry left (decidedly less hairy), Fiona got to work winding, braiding and tying the strands of his hair.

By the last threading treatment, Fiona had managed to secretly create a good, strong rope.

Astonished with how he looked, Prince Harry examined the backs of his hands, his arms, his legs—all hairless. He felt cold and bare, but also free and light. "What shall we do now, Fiona?" the prince asked.

Fiona knew exactly what she planned to do the moment the prince left her room that night. She knew what she had to do—even though the thought of it terrified her. "What do you mean, Prince Harry? You will live a charmed life now, here at the castle, of course."

He looked at her strangely. "But I don't want to stay here, Fiona."

"It's . . . it's . . . your home."

Harry took a deep breath. "It's where I live, Fiona." Then his voice dropped low. "But it's not my home. Hasn't been since my mom died. The king? He barely notices me."

"Even now that you don't have . . . the hair?"

"Even now." Prince Harry lowered his head. "Turns out it wasn't my hair that he didn't care for." Prince Harry looked out the small window into the night sky and sighed. "I'd much rather take my chances out there than in this dreadful castle, where I know I'm not loved. I'm glad that shoe brought you here, Fiona. Brought us together."

Fiona's heart twisted, for she knew that even though she and her father had so little, he loved her deeply. When her mother passed, the bond between Fiona and her father became thicker than the best molasses.

Fiona reached out and touched the prince's hairless hand. "Then all of this was for nothing?"

"Not nothing," the prince said. "I learned something from it. Not a cheerful something, but something important nonetheless. And that matters, Fiona."

That sad truth hung in the air between them.

"Well," Fiona finally said. "For what it's worth, Prince Harry, I care about you, with or without your hair."

"I know that to be true," Harry said, but still he looked terribly sad.

Fiona had a feeling that the truth about the prince's father was more painful to him than the hours and days of the difficult threading procedure. She opened her mouth to tell him about the hair rope she'd fashioned, but then she clamped her lips shut before she ruined her one chance to escape and find her way back home to her father.

"I'd better go to bed, I suppose," the prince said. "I'll ask the cook to make you and Lucky something wonderful for the morning meal."

This made Fiona feel extra guilty. She knew she wouldn't see Prince Harry in the morning. In fact, she'd never see him again. Still, Fiona gave the briefest of nods.

With that, Prince Harry left her prison chamber.

Fiona forced herself to wait twenty slow breaths before pulling the stone away and taking out the hair rope. She gave it a few tugs to test its mettle. Fiona was amazed at the strength of something as weak as a strand of hair, when it was braided together with others.

Lucky barked his excitement.

"Shhh, boy." Fiona ruffled his scruffy fur and realized that without being able to wash at the river for so many days, she must be pretty scruffy and dirty herself. "We'll be home soon, Lucky, and you can bark all you want." The thought made her giddy.

Fiona tied one end of the hair rope to the iron handle on the door and she threw the other end out the window. It was such a long, long way down, but the rope made it nearly to the bottom. Fiona and Lucky would have to jump a ways to the ground. She took a deep breath for bravery. "We can do this!"

Lucky shimmied.

Fiona scooped him into her arms. "Goodbye, dark, dank castle. Goodbye, dear Prince Harry. I wish you well."

With that, Fiona held tight to the hair rope with her right hand and held Lucky to her chest with her left. Then she hoisted herself up and over the window ledge.

The next part, Fiona knew, would not be easy. But worthwhile things rarely were.

A swift wind blew them slightly and took Fiona's breath away.

"Steady, steady," she told her little dog, but really she was trying to calm herself.

Suddenly, the rope jerked. Fiona held tight to Lucky, the rope and her courage. Unexpectedly, they dropped a couple feet, dangling way above the ground. When things steadied, Fiona gathered herself and looked up, expecting to see a castle guard with a sharp spear, ready to cut the hair rope with one strong swipe, surely sending her and Lucky plunging to their doom. Instead, she saw Prince Harry peering over the window ledge.

"What are you doing, Fiona?" he whispered loudly. "I came back to your room to tell you how much I appreciate what you've done for me. Then I saw . . . I saw . . ."

"I'm . . . um . . . we're . . . uh . . ." She and Lucky dangled in the wind against the castle wall.

"You're leaving!" the prince cried.

"Ah . . . eh . . ."

"Without me!"

In that moment, gripping the hair rope for all she was worth, Fiona understood that sometimes princes needed rescuing, too. She hollered up, hoping the wind would swallow most of the sound from her words so no guards would be alerted. "If you're sure you want to do this, Prince Harry, wait until Lucky and I are safely on the ground, then climb down after us. This rope is strong, but it won't hold all our weights at once."

It was then Harry realized the rope hanging out the window, the one attached to the metal handle on the door that had kept him from being able to open it easily, was made from hair—human hair. His human hair. And in that instant, Harry understood that Fiona was clever and resourceful. But was she a true friend? "You're not going to run off and leave me the moment you touch down. Are you?"

"Of course not, Prince Harry. Why would I do that? Now, let me get Lucky down this thing before he pees on me."

Prince Harry couldn't help but laugh.

When Fiona reached the end of the rope, she said a silent prayer, then leapt to the ground. She and Lucky made it. With solid earth beneath her, Fiona didn't dare breathe. She hoped Lucky had the good sense not to bark, not even to whimper, because if a castle guard got wind of them, it would be the end for sure. In fact, Fiona had an overwhelming urge to run—to get as far away from the castle as she could, under cover of darkness, and wend her way home.

Instead of running, though, Fiona looked up.

She saw Harry's butt. He was climbing down. And she knew she couldn't abandon him.

When Harry jumped from the rope and hit bottom with his bottom, he scrambled up quickly. "This way," he whispered. "I know how to get across the moat without alerting the guards. It's how I escaped last time." There was a mischievous twinkle in his green eyes.

Fiona followed closely, quietly.

Prince Harry laid a series of planks across the moat.

Fiona thought he was quite a clever boy.

They ran across the planks and into the woods, but Fiona didn't feel safe until they'd put an hour's worth of desperate running between the castle and themselves, when the only sounds they heard were night noises in the forest and their own heavy breathing.

"Are you frightened?" Fiona asked.

Prince Harry puffed out his chest. "Of course not."

But Fiona could tell he was. "It'll be okay. It's a long way off, but we'll make it together. Right, Lucky?"

Lucky wagged his tail.

And the trio tromped through forest and field until they came upon Fiona's home.

It was full daylight now.

Fiona's father was wandering along a row of cabbages, looking dazed.

"Father!" Fiona called. She ran to him swift and sure, the way an arrow flies to its target.

He looked startled and shocked, then relieved. He scooped up his daughter and pressed his face into her hair. "Oh, my precious girl. I thought I'd lost you, too." He wept openly.

Fiona wiped his tears with the bottom of her filthy, raggedy apron. "Father, I've brought a friend to stay with us."

"A friend?"

"Yes. This is, um, Harry. He has no place else to go."

Fiona glanced at Prince Harry to make sure this was okay to say.

He gave a quick nod.

"Well then," Fiona's father said to the prince. "Let this be your humble home and may we be your family."

And they were—laughing and working and eating and playing together for years and years to come.

Even though Prince Harry thought someone might (maybe hoped someone might), no one from the castle ever came looking for him. And when all his hair grew back the way it was before, he let it be, because he knew Fiona, her father and Lucky loved him just as he was.

He was right, of course.

And they all lived hairily, er, happily ever after.

The End

That was Amy's favorite part of the story, the happily-ever-after before the end.

The Second Happily-Ever-After

Three weeks later, Miles climbed into the passenger seat of the orange Buckington Bowl van. His mom was driving. His dad was back at the lanes, cooking the special menu Miles created. Even his sister had come home to help out. Mercedes was behind the desk at that moment, thumbing through one of Mom's magazines.

Everything had been set up. Everything was ready.

Except Miles. He'd never been more nervous, but he knew this was exactly the right thing. He looked up, took a breath and silently thanked his grandpop, because if Pop hadn't said no to the Bowling Hall of Fame trip, this wouldn't have happened.

The first stop for the Buckington Bowl van was Eternal Peace Funeral Home.

Miles rang the doorbell.

Two men came to the door. Miles recognized them from the funeral and had to swallow hard. "Is, um, Amy home?"

"Ames!" her father shouted.

"Hello, Miles," her uncle Matt said.

Miles nodded. "Hi."

Amy was wearing jeans, a Chicago Cubs sweatshirt that used to belong to her mom, and her sneakers as she came barreling down the stairs. "Yeah?"

"Someone here to see you," her dad said.

"Miles?" Amy could see the Buckington Bowl van outside. Miles was wearing a dapper navy suit and a tie, along with his bowling shoes.

Miles took one look at Amy and blurted out the whole thing: "I'm sorry I couldn't take you to the dance because of what happened to Randall but I made another dance and I want to take you there right now okay?"

Amy stepped back. "Excuse me?"

"Just come with me." Miles pointed to the van, which Amy thought looked like a giant pumpkin. "Please."

Amy looked at her dad. "Okay if I go?"

Her dad nodded. "Of course, Ames."

"Do I need to bring anything?" Amy asked Miles. "Should I change?"

"Nope. It's all been taken care of."

"Hmm. Okay. Bye, Dad. Bye, Uncle Matt."

"Have fun," Uncle Matt said.

"Don't be home too late," her dad warned. "Make sure you're back at a reasonable time."

Just be home by midnight, sweets. Her mom's voice floated into her mind.

"I will." Amy smiled and followed Miles outside into the warm spring air.

Settled in the van, Amy felt her phone vibrate. She glanced at a new message from Kat.

Can't believe I'll be visiting you next week!!!

Amy texted quickly.

It's going to be so great!

As soon as Amy put her phone away, it vibrated again.

This time, it was a funny picture of Ernest in a baby pool filled with colorful plastic balls. Their old neighbor Pam had texted:

Having a ball with Ernest. Ha ha. Wish you were here.

Amy let out a breath. Ernest wasn't with her anymore, but he was with someone who was taking good care of him. He was with someone who enjoyed him and appreciated him. He was with someone who still sent photos and updates regularly.

Amy started to text *Wish I were there, too,* but then she looked over at Miles and deleted those words. They weren't the right ones anymore. Instead, she texted something different:

Looks like fun. Give Ernest a hug for me.

"Everything okay?" Miles asked.

"Actually," Amy said, putting her phone away, "everything's pretty terrific."

Amy saw the tips of Miles's ears turn bright pink.

On the next stop, they picked up Tate. She was wearing the blue dress she was supposed to wear for the school dance and a pair of sparkly blue Converse sneakers. She'd left her penguin hat at home.

When Tate got into the van, she said hello to Miles's mom, then winked at Miles. "Oh, hi, Amy," she said.

"Hey there," Amy replied. Then she turned to Miles. "I'm definitely underdressed for whatever we're going to do."

Miles grinned. "Don't worry. You're perfect."

Amy shivered from her forehead to her feet from Miles's compliment.

They picked up Randall from his house.

"How're you feeling?" Miles's mom asked Randall as soon as he climbed in.

"Really good," Randall said, then patted his pocket. "But I carry two inhalers now . . . just in case."

The kids joked and laughed the whole way to Buckington Bowl.

Miles hopped from the van first and held his hand out to help Amy.

She took his hand and whispered, "My Prince Charming."

"Huh?" Miles said

"N-nothing," she stammered. "Never mind."

Miles led Amy toward Buckington Bowl.

There was a sign on the automatic glass doors: "Closed tonight for a private event."

Inside the bowling center, Miles let go of Amy's hand. She stood there with Miles beside her, and her jaw dropped.

Buckington Bowl had been transformed.

The place was dim, so the new carpet sparkled like a starry night sky. A disco ball overhead cast rainbow bits of light. Music played through crisp, clear speakers.

"What is this?" Amy asked, turning in a circle.

"It's for you," Miles said.

"Me?"

"Yes," Miles said. "You deserve to have a dance, Amy Silverman. So I made one for you." Then Miles looked over at his mom and sister, who were behind the counter. "The box, please."

Mercedes handed a shoe box to Miles.

He took it. "Come with me, Amy."

The pair, followed closely by Tate and Randall and Mercedes and Miles's mom, walked to the snack bar. Miles's dad was already there. So was Stick. He had a big white box with a giant red bow sitting on his lap.

Amy gripped Miles's fingers like Tate might grip a barbell. "Miles, what's going on?"

"You'll see," Miles said. "Stick, please do the honors."

Stick rolled close to Amy. "I, Farley G. Mathers, aka Stick, present to you, dearest Amy, this handmade gift from my tailor shop. I hope it fits. Amen."

Everyone laughed.

Amy's hands trembled as she accepted the box.

Inside was a dress lovelier than the one Cinderella wore to the ball.

"You made this?" Amy asked, pressing the dress's silky silver fabric to her cheek.

"I did," Stick said.

"For me?"

"None other," he replied.

Amy blinked back tears. "It's . . . it's . . . beautiful!"

"Now, now," Stick said. "It ain't nothing but a dress, is all. Go on and change into it so we can all admire you."

Tate joined Amy in the bathroom to help her into the new dress.

"Oh my gosh, it's amazing," Tate said. "See all this lacework? And the sequins?"

"I know," Amy said. "It's just like in the fairy tale." Then Amy looked down at her feet. Her black-and-lime-green sneakers did not go with the fabulous dress. "I can't walk out there wearing these."

Tate grinned.

"What?"

"*What* what?" Tate pressed her fingers to her lips, as though to keep from saying something she shouldn't.

"Oooh, pretty. What color is that on your nails?" Amy asked.

Tate smiled. "It's called 'I Danced the Night Away Gray.' "

Amy nodded, wishing she'd polished her nails.

"Come on, Ames." Tate grabbed her elbow. "Everyone's waiting."

"But . . ." Amy allowed Tate to pull her out of the

bathroom, even though she felt a bit self-conscious about her sneakers.

Everyone oohed and aahed at Amy's new dress.

"Wow," Miles said. "You look . . ." He shook his head. "Come on. Let's go." He led her to lane 48. "Please have a seat."

Amy sat carefully, so as not to ruin her new dress.

Miles sat on a chair facing her, and everyone crowded close by.

"Here." Miles put the shoe box on Amy's lap.

"Another gift?"

Miles nodded.

Amy took the lid off the box and pulled out two bowling shoes—size 8-1/2. The right shoe had a heel lift built in. *A heel lift!*

A tear slipped down Amy's cheek, then another.

"Oh, I didn't mean to make you sad."

Amy shook her head. "You didn't, Miles." She held the shoe with the heel lift to her heart. "Oh, you didn't."

"I, um, noticed how your hip looked like it hurt when you bowled with house shoes, and—"

"Stop," Amy said.

"Stop?"

"They're perfect, Miles." Tears dripped off Amy's chin. She took off her sneakers and slipped her feet into the new bowling shoes. A tingle zinged from her feet to her forehead.

Miles helped her tie them. Then she held up her feet, and everyone cheered.

Then Amy and Miles, dressed in their finest, bowled a game together on lane 48.

No, Dear Reader, Miles did not bowl his perfect game. Not yet, anyway. Because even made-up stories need some truth to their spines.

Don't you agree?

Besides, "perfect" is highly overrated. We can enjoy our messy, imperfect lives so much more when we simply live in the moment, filled with gratitude for exactly what is.

Now, shall we see how this all ends?

When the bowling was done and snacks had been eaten, the lights in the bowling center got even dimmer and the disco ball seemed to grow brighter. Miles's dad put a slow dance song on to play through the crisp new speakers.

Miles held his hand out to Amy. "May I have this dance?" He hoped he remembered all the things Mercedes had taught him about dancing.

"Why, of course," Amy said, feeling like Cinderella. She was glad to be wearing bowling shoes, though, instead of glass slippers.

Amy and Miles danced together under the glittering disco ball.

Miles looked up. "You don't think that thing could fall on us and crush us to death, do you?"

Amy pulled Miles closer.

He stopped talking. Stopped worrying. Miles realized that since he and Amy had been hanging out more, he'd been worrying less. It was almost like Amy helped rescue him from himself.

They got into a rhythm of moving from one side to the other, perfectly aligned.

Amy thought back to the Unitarian Universalist church, where her father had given a wonderful sermon about enjoying each moment in life. At the end of the service, her dad led the congregation in singing "Let It Be a Dance."

> Let it be a dance we do.
> May I have this dance with you?
> Through the good times and the bad times, too,
> Let it be a dance.

Amy remembered the congregation swaying and smiling. She'd looked over at her mom, who had her eyes closed. Moving to the music, she looked so happy.

That was how Amy felt now, dancing in Miles's arms, enjoying every single thing about the moment.

The whirring of a camera startled her.

Amy and Miles looked over and saw Tate with her instant camera, waving a photo. "Oh, this'll be a good one."

"They're almost as cute as us." Randall wrapped an arm around Tate's waist.

"Almost." Tate leaned her head on Randall's shoulder.

When the photo developed, Tate showed Miles and Amy how happy they looked dancing together. Then she passed the photo around. Mercedes was the last person to see it.

"I know exactly where this belongs," Mercedes said. "If it's okay with you, Tate."

Tate nodded. Then everyone followed Mercedes to the "Greatest Stories Ever Bowled" bulletin board, where she grabbed a pushpin from the edge and put the photo of Miles and Amy right in the center, filling up the empty space.

Stick raised his drink. "Hear, hear!"

"Hear, hear!" everyone cheered.

"To Miles and Amy," Miles's dad said, wrapping an arm around his wife's shoulders and pulling her close.

"To Miles and Amy!" everyone shouted.

And they all lived (and bowled) happily ever after.

Epilogue

"*Louise?*"

"*Right here, Billy.*"

"*You look . . . you look—*"

"*I look like you remember me from that first day, Billy. The day I walked into Buckington Bowl with my girlfriends.*"

"*Yes. Yes!*" *Billy said, marveling at what he was seeing.*

"*Billy, this is Mary Jane—that dear girl Amy's mom. She likes to be called Jane.*"

Billy blinked, blinked, blinked. "You're Amy's mom?"

She held out a hand to him. "Yes. It's so nice to meet you, Billy."

He shook Jane's hand. Then he looked down at the

scene below and then back up at Louise. "The kids—
they're getting along just fine without us. Aren't they?"

Louise smiled and nodded. "Yes, Billy. But we still
need to keep an eye on things."

"Oh, don't we, though," Jane said.

"Louise," Billy said. "Do you hear that music?" He
looked over at Jane and saw her with her eyes closed,
swaying. "Louise, they're playing our song."

"Why, Billy Spagoski, if I didn't know better, I'd
think you were asking me to dance."

A wild grin spread across Billy's face. "May I have
the honor, my darling?"

She inhaled deeply. "I've waited a long time for this
moment."

Billy wrapped his wife in a warm embrace, cheek
pressed against cheek, and danced an eternity with the
woman he would always love.

Let it be a dance we do.
May I have this dance with you?
Through the good times and the bad times, too,
Let it be a dance.

Author's Note

Stories often come from a writer's life.

When I was ten, the doctor diagnosed my mom with breast cancer. She needed surgery and would be in the hospital for about a week afterward to recover.

This was particularly scary for me because my parents were divorced, and I lived with my mom and one older sister. I depended on my mom for everything and became terrified of what might happen to me if she died.

While Mom was in the hospital, my dad came and brought me to the market to help buy groceries for my sister and me. I told him the things Mom usually bought, and we put them into the cart. In the cereal aisle, I chose one box of cereal and tossed it in.

Dad said, "Get a couple more boxes. We don't know exactly how long your mom will be in the hospital."

I didn't want more boxes of cereal (although more boxes of sugary cereal is all I ever asked for when I went shopping with Mom). I wanted exactly the number of boxes

Mom let me get every time we went shopping together: one. We didn't have money for more, and Mom didn't like us eating food that wasn't good for us.

I should have been excited to finally load the cart with boxes of any kind of cereal I wanted. But at that moment, all I really wanted was Mom home again and healthy.

My dad threw a couple more boxes into the cart and said, "Let's go."

He'd chosen exactly the kinds of cereal we weren't supposed to eat: the kind with food dyes, loaded with sugar.

Everything felt wrong.

By the time Dad and I got to the checkout line, I was hunched over, crying.

"What's wrong?" asked the woman checking out our groceries.

I turned away, wishing I could disappear. I was embarrassed to be so sad in public.

Dad asked loudly, "What're you crying for?"

Had he already forgotten that Mom was in the hospital, getting surgery for cancer? Had he forgotten there was a chance she could die? That I wouldn't have a mom anymore?

I glared at him and didn't answer. He should have known why I was so upset.

After Mom's surgery, treatments with radiation, and a

long recovery period, she went back to work and back to taking care of me and my sister.

I felt like the luckiest person in the world to have my mom there to keep me safe and raise me, to help me with the hard things and celebrate the wonderful things.

My mom lived until I was twenty-nine and pregnant with my husband's and my younger son. Her cancer had come back for a third time, and she didn't win that final fight. But I counted myself fortunate that my mom lived as long as she did.

Several years ago, our younger son, now an adult, brought home a wonderful girlfriend. She was a delight in our lives. After a while, we learned that when she was eleven, her mom died from cancer.

That information hit me like a punch to the gut. She had experienced the terrible reality I was so afraid of when I was about that same age.

How did she deal with such sadness and grow up to become such a lovely, giving person? What would my life have been like if my mom had died when I was ten or eleven? Who would have taken care of me?

Those questions set me on the path to writing the story you just read. Questions are often the start of stories for me.

How would this feel?
What would happen if . . . ?

The stories I write are my exploration of those questions and my search for answers.

As a reader, you bring your own experiences and curiosity to a story. I hope you found some answers here . . . and maybe some questions that might lead you to further explore and create your own stories.

Acknowledgments

FRAME ONE: To the memory of my mom, Myrna Levin, who read me fairy tales and taught me to thumb my nose when I bowled; who taught me by example to enjoy cooking, reading, hiking through parks, and browsing public library shelves. My mom was always someone I could count on. Always. A single, working parent, Mom was a smart, strong, creative woman who showed me what it meant to be resilient when faced with life's challenges. Her love and spirit live on, especially in my sister, Ellen; niece, Nicole; and nephew, Kyle; and in her best friend, Maxine, from her Tuesday-night bowling league at Facenda Whitaker Lanes.

FRAME TWO: To my agent, Tina Dubois of ICM Partners, who has bowled me over with her brilliant, book-filled head and heart since we began working together in 2005. I can't think of anyone I'd rather have on my team. Tina is in a league of her own when it comes to supporting her diverse list of authors with everything she's got.

Frame Three: To my editor, Kelsey Horton, for taking me on and then cheering me on. Thanks for pushing me beyond where I thought I could take this story. This tale is richer for your deep, thoughtful suggestions. And thanks for coming up with the title. To Beverly Horowitz and the entire team at Delacorte Press/Random House Children's Books, who make literary miracles happen every day: Thank you for everything you do to get good books into the hands of kids who need them most. I'm filled with gratitude for your support of me and my work for well over a decade.

Frame Four: To Crystal Allen, who wrote the world's funniest, most heartfelt bowling book, *How Lamar's Bad Prank Won a Bubba-Sized Trophy*. I dare you not to laugh until you cry when you read the scene about the chocolate-covered peanuts. Seriously! Read it. I'll wait. . . . Crystal is one of the most generous people I know. One of her many generous acts was donating a scholarship so someone could attend a workshop at Bethany Hegedus's magical Writing Barn in Austin, Texas. I'm so glad Crystal and I connected at the Erma Bombeck Writers' Workshop in 2010 and continue to be friends through our writing journeys. I'll never forget our falling-over-funny dinner in Houston with the lovely Laura Ruthven.

Frame Five: To Jane Jergensen, who gave me her 180 bowling badge to inspire my writing of this book and who shared a fun game of bowling with me when we were both in Texas with Kay Hawkins during my school visits. Thank you both for not laughing at me when I bowled.

FRAME SIX: For help with research, a big bouquet of thanks to Pam Collins for chatting with me about her type 1 diabetes journey with her awesome son, even though the story changed to be about something else entirely, as stories often do. And to Mandy Munyan, Family Service Counselor at Aycock-Riverside Funeral and Cremation Center in Jupiter, Florida, for giving me a tour and answering my many questions.

FRAME SEVEN: To Pam, Klaus, and Nico Meyer for providing a quiet place for me to write for a few days when I was stuck on one of the early versions of this book. And to my writing buddy and über-talented author-and-performer friend extraordinaire, Jill Nadler (aka Riley Roam from pageturneradventures.com), who joined me on that mini writing retreat and asked the right questions and made the right suggestions to get me unstuck. Thank you for always being there with wise words, something funny to keep me laughing, a big hug, or a mug of hot tea and a cupcake. You're the best, Jill!

FRAME EIGHT: To Chris Hardwick, who had the most inspiring interview with his late dad, pro bowler Billy Hardwick, on his "The Nerdist" podcast. I listened to that interview over and over. It was just the thing to help give this story life in its early stages.

To my dear father-in-law, Jake, who inspired the character of Billy Spagoski and who inspired me in all the important ways. Thank you for being such a wonderful grandfather to our sons. We all love and miss you, Dad.

To my dad, Jack, whose bowling trophies littered our garage throughout my childhood. The black-and-white photo of him on his Philadelphia bowling league team still hangs in our home.

FRAME NINE: To Elysa Graber-Lipperman and Amelia for sharing your guys' wonderful, nerdy bowling stories, which were the seeds that started this whole thing growing.

To Jeanne, my friend since we were fourteen and getting in trouble in Mr. Perry's science class at Woodrow Wilson Junior High School. Thanks for a million things, including sharing your middle and maiden names with my character Amy in this book. Longtime friends are such a treasure. Right, Addam and Paul?

To my friend Gail Gabert for sharing her stories of growing up in a family that owned a bowling center.

And to Elizabeth Owosinaes for helping me with my other work so I could focus on writing. Thanks also for being my exercise buddy and sharing many long walks/

talks with me through wild woods. I think I owe you a hot chocolate, friend.

To my cherished friends and family who have supported me in a thousand different, vital ways: My love for you all goes deep.

FRAME TEN: To Dan, who has bowled me over every day since we met thirty years ago in northeast Philly. (Thanks for connecting us, Addam!) It's been an honor to experience life's journey with you. You're such a deeply caring, big-hearted, and interesting person. Thanks for always surprising me in the best kinds of ways. And thanks, sweets, for taking such good care of the real world while I toiled for so many, many months on this fictional one.

To our sons, Andrew and Jake: I'm privileged to be your mom.

Andrew, thank you for the time you took to read this story and offer such substantive suggestions. You're an eagle-eyed editor!

Glossary

American Wheelchair Bowling Association (awba.org): An organization that promotes the abilities of wheelchair bowlers.

anchor: The last bowler in a team lineup.

approach: The space extending back from the foul line, used to make the steps and delivery.

average: The score of all games, divided by the number of games.

ball return: A rack for bowling balls at the start of a bowling lane, where the balls are sent after returning from the pinsetter.

bumpers: Removable blockades that prevent gutter balls.

gutter ball: A bowling ball that rolls into a channel on either side of the lane and doesn't hit any pins.

handicap: An adjustment in scores to equalize competition by adding pins on a predetermined basis.

house ball: A bowling ball provided by the bowling center.

lane: A sixty-foot-long wooden alley for the game of tenpins.

league play: Organized competition for team play.

perfect game: Scoring twelve strikes in a row (300 points).

pin: Bowling pins are the target of a bowling ball in games of tenpins. They are usually made from maple wood and a coating. Once in use, pins last about six months before needing to be patched or recoated and another six months before breaking.

pocket: The desirable location for the ball to hit the pins to maximize strike potential.

pumpkin: A ball thrown without spin that hits a pin or pins softly.

scratch: Actual score, without the benefit of a handicap.

spare: Achieved when a player knocks down the pins left standing after the first throw with the second throw.

strike: Achieved when a player knocks down all ten pins with the first throw.

turkey: Three consecutive strikes.

WRITING AND STORY TERMS

character: A person in a story.

climax: The point of highest dramatic tension in a story, or a major turning point in the action.

dialogue: Conversation between two or more characters.

fiction: A story invented by the imagination.

foreshadow: To represent or indicate beforehand what will happen in the future.

hero: The principal male character in a story.

heroine: The principal female character in a story.

inciting incident: An event that sets the plot of a story in motion. This usually occurs after the background and setting have been given.

mood: A distinctive atmosphere.

narrator: One who tells a story; one who provides spoken commentary for a story.

outline: A plan for or a summary of a story.

plot: The events that make up a story.

plot twist: A change in the expected outcome or direction of a story.

point of view: A character's position, or the perspective from which narration is presented.

resolution: The point in a story at which the chief dramatic complication is worked out.

rewrite: To write again, especially in an improved form.

setting: The time and place of the action of a story.

tone: The style or manner of expression in a story.

About the Author

Donna Gephart's award-winning novels are packed with humor and heart. They include *Lily and Dunkin; Death by Toilet Paper; Olivia Bean, Trivia Queen; How to Survive Middle-School;* and *As if Being 12¾ Isn't Bad Enough, My Mother Is Running for President!* Donna is a popular speaker at schools, conferences, and book festivals. For reading guides, resources, writing tips, and more, visit donnagephart.com.